# KNIGHTS OF THE BAR 10

When Gene Adams and his riders of the Bar 10 arrive in the town of McCoy with their prime steers, they find the pens filled with Circle O and Lazy J stock, leaving less cash for their beeves. But corrupt cattle agent Roscoe Martin has hired a gunfighter to rob the weary Circle O and Lazy J boys of their money on their way home. Adams and his men saddle up in a bid to warn their rivals. They are no longer just cowboys: they are the Knights of the Bar 10.

BOYD CASSIDY

◆

# KNIGHTS OF THE BAR 10

*Complete and Unabridged*

# LINFORD
*Leicester*

First published in Great Britain in 2015 by
Robert Hale Limited
London

First Linford Edition
published 2017
by arrangement with
Robert Hale
an imprint of The Crowood Press
Wiltshire

A catalogue record for this book is available
from the British Library.

ISBN 978–1–4448–3160–3

Published by
F. A. Thorpe (Publishing)
Anstey, Leicestershire

Set by Words & Graphics Ltd.
Anstey, Leicestershire
Printed and bound in Great Britain by
T. J. International Ltd., Padstow, Cornwall

This book is printed on acid-free paper

*Dedicated to my friends
in Grass Valley, California.*

# Prologue

Every animal upon the tree-covered hillside suddenly became silent. It was as though the sight and putrid scent of the intruders warned them to become as quiet as possible until the riders passed through. Each of the devilish horsemen had the scent of death lingering upon him. These were no normal drifters who had penetrated the very heart of the tree-covered hills. These were men who lived for the thrill of death itself.

Killing had become an addiction and, like all addictions, it controlled them as would an unseen master. Whatever humanity they had once possessed was long gone. Now they were ravenous creatures who barely resembled normal men.

Each of them had tasted the blood of brutal slaughter and had developed a craving for it. It was a craving that could never be satisfied, no matter how many times they repeated the savage act.

The dust filtered through the brush and swept down into the draw as the six heavily armed riders trailed their leader out into the blazing sun and tasted its merciless heat. They all drew rein and stopped their lathered-up mounts at the edge of the sun-bleached chasm. They leaned upon their saddle horns and eased their backsides off the shining leather of their saddles. The seven horsemen remained silent as they felt the violent sun start to blister their exposed flesh. Each pulled the brim of his Stetson down to shield his face from the burning rays as the lead rider looped a leg over the neck of his mount before sliding to the ground beside its shoulder.

These were no ordinary horsemen.

They were the most deadly of creatures. Men cast out from society and feared by all who had ever heard of them. Only their leader was known by name. The rest were his deadly henchmen. Vermin who did as they were commanded without guilt or mercy.

Yet even when they did the bloody bidding of their leader none of them could equal his evil exploits. Few men could have ever imagined the horrors he had perpetrated over the ten years he had roamed the West. For only a mind as sick and demented as that of Buffalo Ben Gardner could envisage such atrocities.

Gardner was built as his nickname implied. Tall and wide and stacked with equal portions of muscle and bulk he stood well over six and a half feet tall and weighed close to 300 pounds.

Some reasoned that Gardner was one of those strange creatures branded as mountain men. His sheer size seemed to indicate that he was bred to rip trees out of the ground with his powerful arms, yet no mountain man had ever been known to kill as freely as he did.

The massive brute stared out at the draw far below their high vantage point. His eyes studied it as though seeking something or someone to destroy next.

He snorted like a brooding bull. A long, unkempt black beard covered most of his barrelled chest and a deep scar traced the length of the right side of his face from the sweat band of his hat down through his eyebrow and across his cheek before disappearing into the black abundance of hair which covered his jaw.

Gardner removed his hat and battered it against his leg as he thought about the reason he was here. Money had drawn him to this place but it was the possibility that once again he and his followers might be able to kill fresh victims that was the true lure.

His black hair fell over his shoulders as sweat flowed down his unnerving features. He felt the sun start to fry the beads of sweat that traced down his monstrous face and he growled. He returned his hat to his head and pulled its brim down to shade his eyes.

Gardner rested one of his massive hands on the mane of his exhausted horse. This was the first time he had ridden this far south and he did not like the unyielding heat. His fingers touched his scar. The wound which had virtually split his face in half had healed badly. For Gardner could neither blink nor close his right eye like most other men. It was permanently open in a never-ending stare. It gave the notorious outlaw an even stranger appearance than nature had already cursed him with.

He swung round and looked at his band of fearful followers.

'Rest these nags,' Gardner snapped loudly. 'We got plenty of time.'

The six exhausted riders dropped from their mounts thankfully. None of them had stopped riding for more than twelve hours as they trailed Gardner, wondering where he was leading them but too scared to ask.

'Take the saddles off their backs,'

Gardner ordered. He raised his own fender and hung the stirrup on his saddle horn. 'We got plenty of time. We'll have us some vittles, and then when the nags are rested we'll carry on.'

The men had no idea where they were headed or what Gardner had planned. Yet not one of them had the guts to enquire. Even the most hardened of souls knew when it was unwise to question a creature like Buffalo.

Gardner loosened his cinch, then buried his stout fingers under the saddle blanket and hauled the hefty weight clear of the horse's back. Steam rose from the lather as Gardner dropped the saddle on to the ground.

'Should we rub the horses down, Buffalo?' one of the men asked.

Buffalo Ben Gardner dismissed the idea.

'The sun will dry these horses good enough.' Gardner spat as he picked up his canteen and unscrewed its stopper.

'Why waste energy?'

One of the outlaws rested his own saddle on the dust. He watched as Gardner drank. Then he ambled up to the massive man and paused beside his horse's tail. Weariness had dampened his fear of the gruesome Gardner.

'I was reckoning that we're headed to McCoy, Buffalo,' Jake Wells said nervously, pulling his tobacco pouch free of his shirt pocket. 'I seem to recognize this territory.'

Gardner lowered the canteen from his mouth. Water dripped from his beard as he stared at Wells. His unblinking eye burned into the outlaw.

'You asking where we're headed, Jake?' the giant of a man growled. 'Are you?'

Wells shook his head. 'Nope. I was just reckoning that if this is the same territory that I rode through ten years back then we must be headed to McCoy.'

Gardner grunted. 'You might be right.'

'Am I?' Wells sprinkled his makings on to the curled cigarette paper in his fingers before rolling it.

'Are you what?'

Wells hung the tobacco pouch from his teeth and turned so that he did not make eye contact with the unpredictable Gardner.

'Am I right or am I just dog-tired and all mixed up?' Wells asked with a shrug.

Gardner dropped the canteen, stepped over his saddle and leant over Wells as the far smaller man ran the gummed edge of his cigarette paper along his tongue. The massive man loomed over Wells and snorted like a bull.

'I told you a hundred times that you boys just follow me and never ask me no questions,' he snapped.

Wells shrugged. 'You sure did tell us, Buffalo. I was just wondering, that's all.'

Faster than any man of his size or build should have been able to move, Gardner grabbed Wells and lifted him off his feet. He hoisted the outlaw aloft and stared up into the eyes of the man he held suspended above him.

Wells did not say a word as his tobacco pouch fell from his mouth and landed on the ground beside Gardner's boots. As though he were carrying a small child, Gardner walked around the tails of their horses, then threw Wells on to the sun-baked ground.

Gardner gave a grunt as he watched Wells roll back down the slope towards him. As the startled outlaw came to a rest at his feet their eyes met.

Winded, Wells spat the dust from his mouth and diverted his eyes to the ground beneath him. A cold chill ran through him, defying the savage heat, when he saw the shadow of the giant man bending over his helpless form. Every bruised bone in his body expected Gardner to draw and fire one of his guns. Then he heard the huge man whisper.

'For your information we're headed some place that ain't called McCoy, Jake,' Gardner hissed like a sidewinder.

'All you and the boys gotta do is follow me. Savvy?'

Like a whipped dog Wells cringed. Then he nodded.

The other outlaws remained between the safety of their horses as Gardner walked back to his mount and sat down upon the ground. Wells crawled back to the rest of the gang before scrambling to his feet. Every one of the six men was shocked that Wells was still alive. They had all seen Gardner kill men for far less than asking a question.

Jake Wells did not dare utter another word.

# 1

The railhead at McCoy was busier than it had been in more than three seasons. The hundreds of stock pens that flanked the tracks were filled to overflowing with steers. Every steer awaited its fate beneath the hot afternoon sun as the first of many trains arrived at the famed cattle town. Clouds of black smoke billowed from their stacks as the hissing iron monsters were guided between the never-ending rows of pens. Soon every one of the various breeds of cattle would be loaded into the freight cars and transported back East for consumption by less hardy souls.

The treacherous journey that the cowboys had undertaken to drive their herds to McCoy meant nothing to the agents when it came to bidding for the stock. All they considered was the fact that the more herds that were brought into McCoy the more the prices were driven down. The Eastern buyers knew only too well that none of the cowboys could refuse their price.

It was take it or leave it. None of the drovers could do anything but accept the price they were quoted.

Three massive cattle drives had all arrived at McCoy at virtually the same time, each of them in a vain bid to get the best price for their beef on the hoof. The sight of so many steers was good for the agents who made their money by buying and selling the vast herds, but not so good for the men who owned the cattle.

The price per head was marked down and that hurt the pockets of the ranchers who arrived later than the first trail drives.

First to arrive always earned top dollar. Second to arrive got slightly less and the last to drive their steers into the pens got whatever the agents offered them.

A despondent Gene Lon Adams rested his jaw on the back of his gloved hands and looked over the fence poles into the dust churned up by the captive steers as they waited to be loaded on to yet another freight train.

For the first time in decades Adams had been delayed in setting out from the Bar 10. Rustlers had struck at his famed ranch but, to his surprise, they had not raided his longhorn steers. They had, however, stolen most of his horses. Without enough fresh mounts it was impossible for Adams to start the cattle drive on time. He and his cowboys had wasted weeks rounding up spare mounts for the long journey north. As a result the Bar 10 herd had arrived in McCoy last of all. It was a bitter pill to swallow but the wide-shouldered Adams knew that he was wealthy enough to withstand the financial loss.

He resolved not to let it happen again, though.

Adams was tired after leading 3,000 longhorns from the Bar 10 to McCoy, but his sore hide was the last of his problems. He had made less than half the money he usually made from the sale of his beef due to the fact that his herd had arrived behind two other cattle drives.

The delay had taught him an expensive lesson. He vowed that he would never need to be taught it again.

The silver-haired rancher watched as the cattle agents moved between the stock pens and instructed the scores of labourers which steers had to be loaded into the freight cars next. As he rubbed the dust from his features he spotted the pinto pony heading towards him. The rider eased his mount as he closed in on the weary rancher.

Johnny Puma dropped down from his pinto and secured his reins to one of the fence poles. He moved next to the troubled rancher and exhaled as he beat the dust from his chaps with his Stetson. The young cowboy could see that Adams was troubled.

'The boys have been saying how quiet you've been since we arrived in town, Gene,' Johnny remarked, placing his hat back over his fine head of hair. 'How come?'

Gene Adams straightened up as he heard his young ranch hand's voice. He looked at Johnny and rested his hand upon the youngster's shoulder.

'Remind me to set off a month earlier next time, Johnny,' he said.

'What you mean?' Johnny asked.

'The Lazy J and the Circle O both got top dollar for their dogies, boy,' Adams told him. 'We arrived third in line and the agents dropped their price.'

'Can they do that?' Johnny queried.

'Sure they can.' Adams forced a smile. 'They weren't desperate for beef to fill their Eastern client's bellies by the time we got these steers penned. We lost a heap of money, Johnny.'

Johnny looked at the ground. 'Reckon

us leaving late didn't help. Next time I'll make sure we have enough horses ready for the drive.'

Adams patted the youngster's back. 'Next time we'll keep every damn horse in the corral by the ranch house. We wasted a lot of time searching for horses to buy for the drive.'

Johnny pulled his leathers free and started to lead the pinto after the long-legged rancher.

'Did you get paid, Gene?'

Adams nodded and patted his shirt pocket. 'I got me a chit here. We'll cash it in before we leave McCoy.'

'Them rustlers sure ruined your drive by stealing our horses,' Johnny remarked. 'We didn't even know the horses were gone until it was too late.'

'The delay cost the Bar 10 thousands of dollars, boy,' Adams explained. 'But how were we to know that they would take our horses to sell to the army? I've never had any horses stolen before. The varmints usually rustle longhorns, not nags.'

The two men walked between the stock pens.

'We lost thousands, Gene?' Johnny asked the tall, silver-haired rancher.

Adams paused and looked at the young man. 'If we'd arrived first or even second we'd have got over twenty bucks a head. I got barely half that.'

Just then two cowboys rode between the stock pens and drew rein near the two men. Adams turned and looked up at the familiar riders. He touched the brim of his ten-gallon hat and nodded.

'Howdy, Matt,' Adams said to the first man. Then he looked at the second rider. 'Joe.'

Brothers Matt and Joe Olsen were the owners of the Circle O ranch and had led their own cattle drive to McCoy. They smiled down at the two Bar 10 men.

'Howdy, Gene.' Matt grinned.

'First time we ever beat the Bar 10 to McCoy, Matt,' Joe said to his brother as he sucked on a cigar. 'Feels good. Feels darn good.'

'Reckon you didn't get top dollar this time, Gene,' Matt Olsen said, grinning.

Johnny frowned angrily. 'What's that meant to mean, Matt?'

Adams placed a fatherly hand on his young friend's shoulder to restrain him.

'Matt don't mean nothing, Johnny. He's just pleased to be able to rub salt in our beans,' Adams said. He looked at the brothers. 'Ain't that right, boys?'

Joe Olsen nodded. 'That's right, Gene. I'm just tickled pink that we got top dollar for our white-faces.'

'You ain't sore are you, Gene?' Matt asked.

'Nope, I'm just a tad poorer than I reckoned on being,' Adams admitted.

Johnny was angry and kicked at the dust. 'Enjoy it while you can, boys. We'll beat you to these pens next time. Next time it'll be the Circle O that draws the short straw.'

Joe turned his horse and spurred. His laughter hung in the afternoon air as he headed away from the rail yard towards the nearest saloon.

The older brother leaned over his saddle horn and smiled at Adams. 'We sure got the drop on you boys this time, Gene. I couldn't hardly believe it when the agents told me that the Bar 10 wasn't even here yet. How come?'

'Josh it up, Matt.' Adams returned the smile and rested his gloved hands on his gun grips. 'You'll be eating our dust on the next drive.'

Matt Olsen teased his reins and turned his mount. 'No hard feelings, Gene. I'll be keeping my boys at the southern end of town until I've paid them off. Maybe it'll be wise if you keep the Bar 10 cowboys at this end of McCoy. I'd hate for there to be any blood spilled.'

'Understood, Matt.' Adams touched his hat brim again.

Olsen tapped his spurs and rode after his brother. Johnny looked at Adams curiously.

'You figuring on us staying out of trouble, Gene?'

Adams started walking again. 'I sure

am, Johnny. The last thing I want is for you and the boys to start trouble with the Circle O boys.'

'But it ain't worth tangling with the Lazy J bunch,' Johnny moaned. 'Most of them are as old as Tomahawk.'

Adams looked all around the stock pens for his ancient friend. 'That reminds me. Where is that old galoot?'

'I reckon he's either drinking, eating or womanizing,' Johnny said with a wry smile on his face. 'I seen him sniffing the air as soon as we guided the steers into town. That old critter can smell hard liquor from half a mile away.'

'You're right, Johnny,' Adams said through gritted teeth. 'That old buzzard is powerful ornery when he's liquored up.'

'If he had any teeth he'd be darn dangerous,' Johnny added.

Adams shook his head. 'When that old varmint starts sniffing at the air all sorts of things can happen. I wonder where that cantankerous critter is?'

As the pair reached the last of the

stock pens the sound of gunshots rang out over the railhead buildings. Adams grabbed the arm of his companion. Gene looked at Johnny.

'That don't sound friendly, Johnny,' he observed.

'That's a heap of serious gunplay, Gene.' Johnny nodded as the shots echoed around them. 'I'm sure happy these steers are penned up, otherwise they might stampede.'

Adams gave a knowing nod, then looked to where he had left his chestnut mare. He started running towards it.

'You ride into town while I get my horse, Johnny,' he shouted over his shoulder. 'For all we know Tomahawk is the one firing his gun. That old fossil can rile a preacher when he's liquored up.'

'It's more likely he's being shot at, Gene.' Johnny grabbed the mane of his pony and swung up on to its saddle. He gathered his reins and spurred.

Adams reached his horse, grabbed his reins and tugged them free of the hitching pole. He stepped into his stirrup and hauled his long frame on to the high-shouldered mare.

'C'mon, Amy,' the rancher said. He pulled his reins to his left and spurred.

# 2

Johnny had stopped his pinto at the edge of the long main street as Gene Adams thundered around a corner and rode through the youngster's dust. The rancher glanced at the cowboy and yelled at him.

'What the hell are you waiting for, Johnny?'

Johnny slapped his long leathers across the tail of the black-and-white horse and chased the determined Adams into the heart of McCoy.

Both riders could smell the acrid scent of gun-smoke lingering in the blinding sunlight as they galloped towards the settlement's array of saloons.

Adams pointed at the Black Ace saloon, abruptly stopped his mare and leapt from his saddle. Johnny watched the rancher stride purposefully into the large saloon. As he came alongside Adams's tall chestnut horse he jumped off his pony.

'Wait up, Gene,' Johnny shouted as he tried to catch up with his boss.

But Gene Adams did not hear his young friend. He had the scent of fresh gunplay in his nostrils as he stepped up on to the boardwalk and pushed his way into the saloon.

The swing doors rocked on their hinges behind the rancher's broad shoulders as he lowered his head and waited for his eyes to adjust to the difference in light.

The Black Ace was half full. More than a hundred people were gathered inside. Adams stood as still as a statue but his fingers flexed above his holstered guns as his eyes darted to each and every face within the saloon.

Some men might have considered that they were in the wrong place. It was quiet, but Adams was not easily taken in. The smell of gunfire remained in the saloon. Even the stink of stale whiskey, beer and tobacco smoke could not fool the legendary rancher.

He knew that this was where the shooting had taken place.

Every face was different but had one thing in common. Each looked frightened by something or someone lurking among them in the drinking hole.

Johnny burst through the swing doors and skidded across the sawdust to come to the side of Adams.

'What's happening, Gene?' Johnny asked, resting his gloved hands on his gun grips.

Adams did not reply. He simply watched the faces of the crowd before him like an eagle studies its prey. A dozen or more bar girls were dotted among the various types of drinking men. They were as sober as judges even though they made most of their money from buying drinks for the men. Adams strode across the barroom towards one of the girls. She was one whom he had known for several years.

When he reached her he stopped. He

was close enough to smell the apple juice on her breath. Without taking his eyes from the scores of customers' faces he spoke to her.

'Who was doing all the shooting, Maisie?' he asked.

The bar girl adjusted her low-cut dress and moved closer to the rancher. Her eyelashes fluttered as she spoke.

'Two *hombres*, Gene,' she whispered from the corners of her painted lips. 'Strangers. I've never seen them in McCoy before.'

'Was anyone hurt?' Adams wondered.

Maisie bowed her head slowly. She pointed at the side wall. Adams turned and glared at a crowd of people. They parted like the biblical Red Sea and allowed the rancher's eyes to focus on the blood which was splattered up the wallpaper. Crimson gore still trailed down its fabric around the bullet holes in the wall.

Adams looked down at the two bodies. Neither was armed but both were dead.

The rancher watched as Johnny swiftly checked the bodies and then came to his side. The youngster wiped the blood from his gloved fingertips.

'Dead, Gene,' Johnny said.

'I already figured that, son.' Adams returned his attention to the bar girl.

'They just cut them down, Gene,' she said. 'There was no call for them to do that but they did it anyway. I heard one of them cuss. They thought them boys were Bar 10 cowboys, Gene.'

'Whoever them two drovers were they didn't belong to the Bar 10, Maisie,' Adams said sadly. 'They're either Circle O or Lazy J hands.'

The woman looked troubled as she pressed her fine body against the rancher and gripped his arm. 'You oughta get your boys out of McCoy, Gene.'

'I've never run away from trouble, girl,' Adams told her in a low drawl. 'I face it head on.'

'Them varmints were looking to kill anyone belonging to the Bar 10, Gene,'

Maisie said with a heavy sigh. 'Pretty soon they'll get it right.'

'Where are they?' Adams quietly enquired.

'They ran out back but warned folks to say nothing or they'd come back and kill them,' she replied. Then she turned away from the rancher and rested her hands on the bar counter.

Adams glanced at Johnny. The look told the youngster to keep watching the faces of the frightened crowd. The rancher swung on his heels and rested his black-gloved hands on the counter, next to Maisie's.

The barman was shaking. He looked terrified.

Adams lifted a nearby bottle and filled a thimble glass full of whiskey. He downed the fiery liquor in one throw, then nodded and moved away from the counter.

'Johnny,' Adams said.

Johnny followed his boss into the crowd. 'Who we looking for, Gene?'

'Strangers in town, son.' Adams

continued walking. The people parted without being told as the Bar 10 men continued towards the back wall.

Johnny flicked the leather loops off his gun hammers in readiness as he kept pace with his tall companion.

'This town is full of strangers, Gene,' he said, his keen eyes darting from one face to the next. 'How on earth are we gonna tell when we meet the right ones?'

'Easy,' Adams said as they reached a door. 'The strangers we're looking for will start shooting at us when we find them, Johnny.'

Johnny sighed and watched as the rancher turned the door handle and pushed the door forward. A powerful arm stopped the young cowboy from walking out of the Black Ace. The youngster looked at Adams.

'What's wrong, Gene?' Johnny asked.

Adams stared into the dark room. It was a room they had both often walked through to the outhouse out back over the years, but this time something was different. Adams sniffed the air.

'I can smell their gunsmoke, Johnny,' Adams warned. 'That means they're either close, with their guns still trailing smoke, or they ain't left the saloon.'

Johnny crouched down and squinted into the dimly lit room. Unlike the large saloon it did not have any windows to allow light into it. Boxes of whiskey were stacked in groups around the room.

'What can you see?' Adams asked, sliding one of his guns from its holster. He cocked its hammer.

Johnny shook his head. 'I don't see or hear anything, Gene.'

Adams did not say anything more. He turned, went back to the barman, then returned.

Johnny rose to his feet as Adams pulled the door towards him and closed it. He slid a key into its lock and turned it. The rancher tossed the key back to the bartender and led his young companion to a side door.

'What we doing, Gene?' Johnny

asked as Adams opened the door that led to the alley. After checking the alley, which led to the rear of the building, was empty he indicated for the cowboy to follow him.

'Get one of your guns ready,' Adams whispered.

Both men moved silently along the sandy alley. The smell of the outhouse filled both men's nostrils. Johnny did as Adams had instructed and pulled one of his six-shooters free of its holster.

They closed the distance between themselves and the back of the Black Ace. The nearer they got the stronger the smell became.

'You'd think they'd have filled the outhouse with some fresh lime,' Adams said, peering carefully round the corner, staring at the outhouse.

Johnny moved to the rancher's side.

'They could be halfway down the street by now, Gene,' he commented.

'They're still around here someplace, boy,' Adams argued.

'How can you be so sure?'

'I'm sure,' Adams said.

Before Johnny could say another word the rancher moved away from him, fast and silent. Adams did not stop until he reached the back door of the saloon, then he pointed his gun at the outhouse.

Johnny quietly moved to the fragrant structure and ripped the door open. It was empty apart from a million flies and a sickening cloud of fumes. The cowboy shut the door and stepped closer to the rancher.

'How do you know they're still around, Gene?' Johnny quietly asked Adams again.

The rancher waved his gun at the saloon yard. Apart from the outhouse and a few empty wooden barrels a ten-foot-high wooden wall surrounded the yard. A sturdy wooden wall, topped with barbed wire. Johnny nodded in agreement.

Adams rested his back to one side of the door as the cowboy took a place against the other.

For a few moments it was silent; then they heard movement inside the storeroom.

Adams touched his lips with the barrel of his .45. Johnny nodded and pressed himself up against the rear wall with one of his trusty guns gripped in his hands.

Both the Bar 10 men listened as the gun-happy strangers moved away from their hiding-places and realized that they were locked out of the Black Ace barroom.

Adams narrowed his eyes.

Suddenly, to the surprise of both the Bar 10 men, the door was flung violently outwards.

# 3

Hot lead spewed from the gun barrels of the two men as they forced their way out into the bright sunshine. Shafts of lethal venom cut through the afternoon air and deafened both Johnny and Adams as they ducked for cover. Luckily for the Bar 10 men, the pair of ruthless gunmen found themselves blinded by the dazzling sunlight as they emerged into the yard. It was in total contrast to the dim interior of the saloon's storeroom, and this gave both Adams and Johnny a few precious seconds to steady themselves.

One of the shooters felt the hands of the young cowboy grab his gun arm. They wrestled before Johnny was knocked off balance and thrown against the rear wall of the saloon. Dazed, the young Bar 10 cowboy swung his gun up and fanned its hammer at both ruthless killers. Dodging lead, they collided with the outhouse and blasted a barrage of bullets at Johnny as the ramshackle structure collapsed into smouldering debris.

The full force of the door had sent the rancher crashing across the yard. The stunned Adams steadied himself as deafening shots cut through the sunlight as they sought him out. The volley of potential death tore chunks of wood from the planks behind Adams. Steadying his tall, lean frame, the rancher fired into the choking gunsmoke at his adversaries.

Then he felt the pain which only those who have tasted lead can ever truly comprehend. One of their bullets ripped through his topcoat and penetrated his body. He spun around as the small lead ball glanced off his ribs.

Agony clawed at the very soul of Adams. Before he knew what had happened he had hit the ground. Still clutching his .45 Adams looked up from the dust and squeezed on his trigger again. The kick from the powerful weapon seemed to vibrate through every muscle in his arm. The tall Texan twisted in the dust. He forced himself up as another few shots sought to add to his misery.

The wooden side wall of the saloon was peppered. Sawdust showered over the wounded rancher as the two deadly killers emerged from the shattered outhouse, fanning their gun hammers feverishly.

Defying the pain which consumed him like boiling oil, Adams forced his bloodied frame away from the back wall of the Black Ace.

A trail of scarlet droplets marked his laboured attempt to escape the unknown gunmen's bullets.

Less than twenty feet away from the valiant Adams, Johnny could see that the gunmen's bullets were closing in on the wounded rancher. He gritted his teeth, narrowed his eyes and shook the debris from his bruised shoulders. He leapt forward like the wild beast after which he was named.

Johnny fired in rapid succession with both his trusty Colts. There was a dogged determination in the young cowboy as he kept advancing on the devilish pair of killers.

'You ain't gonna add any more notches to them guns of yours, boys,' he growled as finally he managed to shake the burning dust from his eyes.

Johnny kicked the last standing wall of the outhouse out of his way, then he felt the impact as a burly shoulder charged into his lean frame.

The Bar 10 cowboy felt himself knocked backwards. His shoulders collided with the ground. He watched his boots trace a trail across the blue sky before they landed back on the dust.

A bullet hit the sand beside his left hand. Dust was kicked up as the two shadows closed in on him. The young cowboy did not wait for a second shot to ring out.

Johnny Puma leapt back to his feet

and squeezed on his triggers with determined wrath burning into his craw. He heard the screams but fired again.

The larger of the pair turned on his heels and fell lifelessly towards him. Like a seasoned Mexican bullfighter, Johnny stepped to his side as the bigger man landed beside his boot.

Knowing that his and Adams's life depended on his ending the brutal fight as quickly as possible, Johnny fired the last of his bullets into the other gunman.

A pathetic groan filled the yard. Johnny narrowed his sore eyes and watched the gunman punched off his feet by the sheer power of the well-aimed bullets.

The gunman flew through the air and crashed head first into the wrecked outhouse. Johnny strode forward and glanced at the sight.

He shook his head.

'Chew on that,' he muttered, and spat at the body. His gloved hands shook the spent casings from both his guns in turn and swiftly reloaded them with fresh bullets from his hand-tooled belt.

As quickly as it had begun, the furious gunfight was over.

Johnny brushed the smouldering dust from his clothing and slowly advanced through the choking smoke. His eyes stared down at the two men. There was no mistaking the sight of death, but Johnny showed no emotion as he kicked the guns from the lifeless hands.

Death was always close to cowboys.

Then, as the dust cleared, Johnny focused on the wounded Adams. The rancher was clutching his side and propping himself up on his elbow as Johnny advanced towards his boss.

He knelt and stared at Adams.

'You OK, Gene?' he nervously asked as his eyes stared at the bloodstained rancher beside him.

Gene Adams could see the concern in the cowboy's face. He grinned and patted Johnny's leg. 'I've been a lot better but by the looks of them two varmints I guess I'm a whole lot luckier than them.'

'Who were they, Gene?' Johnny asked.

'I didn't recognize them, son,' Adams said as he clutched his side.

'And why'd they kill them two critters in the saloon?' Johnny wondered. 'It don't make no sense. No sense at all.'

'It sure don't,' Adams agreed.

Johnny assisted the rancher back to his feet and patted him down. Suddenly both men heard movement behind them in the alley. They turned. Johnny drew his gun and cocked it.

'Somebody's coming, Gene,' he drawled.

'I sure hope it's a doctor with a heap of catgut,' said the rancher, and he sighed as he glanced down at the blood seeping from between his gloved fingers. 'This leak needs stemming.'

Johnny pointed his gun at the two dead men before turning it again to the sound of the approaching footsteps.

'It also might be friends of them dead 'uns, Gene,' he said.

The tall rancher bit his lip thoughtfully.

'You might be right, Johnny. I hadn't thought about that.'

Adams wrapped his arm around the cowboy's shoulder to steady his tall frame. He stared through the gunsmoke, looking towards the corner of the saloon. The sound of footsteps grew louder.

# 4

Both Bar 10 men sighed in relief when they saw the familiar faces of Happy Summers and Rip Calloway coming round the corner of the Black Ace. Johnny holstered his gun and supported the tall rancher as they looked at the pair of confused cowhands. Both wranglers stopped in their tracks and looked at the dead bodies lying between Adams, Johnny and themselves. The wounded rancher started forward towards his two cowboys, using Johnny as a crutch.

'I wondered where you boys were,' Adams said.

Rip slid his six-shooter back into its holster and watched as Adams was guided towards them.

'We heard the shooting and someone told us they seen you two entering the saloon, Gene,' he said. 'We figured we'd come and help you boys out.'

'You're a tad late, Rip,' Johnny told him.

Adams moved cautiously. Every step was agony. The pain of every movement was carved into his face. 'Leastways they tried to help us, Johnny.'

'You OK, Gene?' Rip asked, seeing the blood still seeping between Adams's gloved fingers as the rancher pressed his hand against his side.

The rancher looked into the concerned wrangler's face and rolled his eyes. 'Do I look OK, Rip? I'm bleeding like a pig, if you ain't noticed.'

Happy rubbed his neck. 'To be honest, you do look darn awful, Gene.'

'I look better than them two,' Adams snapped, pointing at the dead killers.

'You do, Gene,' Rip agreed. 'You look a whole lot better than them.'

Happy moved to Gene's side and looked at the bodies. 'Them varmints look plumb pitiful, now you mention it.'

'Get me to the doc's, Johnny,' Adams whispered. Then he glanced at the two cowboys. 'You boys can find out who them dead varmints were. Savvy? I wanna know their identities.'

Rip looked baffled. 'Why? They're both dead. What use is it to know their names?'

'Hell. One of them got his head down the privy, Gene,' Happy complained to his boss. 'Are you sure you wanna know who they are?'

The wounded rancher narrowed his eyes at the cowboy.

'Yep, I'm damn sure, Happy,' Adams railed as Johnny helped him down the alley towards the main street. 'I also wanna know if they were working for someone. See if they got paper on them.'

'What kinda paper, Gene?' Happy asked.

'Paper with a name scrawled on it,' Adams shouted over his, shoulder. 'Anything that'll give us a clue as to why two drifters started killing.'

Reluctantly, Rip and Happy walked slowly towards what was left of the outhouse. Neither was in any hurry to get there as the stench wafted over them.

'He sure looks real messed up, Rip,' Happy noted as they hovered above the half-submerged body.

Rip nodded. 'Reckon we best check the other one first, Happy. He's a darn sight cleaner than his partner.'

Both cowboys turned the dead stranger over. His lifeless eyes looked up into the blazing sun as both Happy and Rip frantically searched his pockets for anything which might satisfy Gene Adams.

Rip was about to concede defeat when his fingers felt something buried deep in the dead man's pants pocket. A thankful smile etched itself across his face.

'Have you found something, Rip?' Happy asked. 'Have you found what Gene told us to look for? I sure don't fancy looking through the pockets of that critter with his head and shoulders in that stinking hole. Have you found something, Rip? Have you?'

Carefully Rip pulled out the paper and unfolded it. He cast his eyes over the words written upon its creased surface.

His smile widened. 'Yep.'

'What is that?'

'A banker's draft, Happy,' Rip said. 'Who'd pay two saddle tramps a hundred dollars? And why?'

# 5

There was only one cowhand on the Bar 10 payroll who seemed to have been there for ever. The cantankerous Tomahawk sat outside the Lucky Spur saloon and squinted into the dust before returning his attention to the unopened bottle of whiskey he had purchased more than two hours earlier. The wily old man sniffed the air, stroked the glass bottle and licked his lips at the sight of the amber liquor it contained. He rested his free hand on the Indian hatchet in his belt and frowned as he saw two familiar riders trotting towards him.

Red Evans and Larry Drake rode their saddle mounts up to the large drinking hole, grinning at the sight of the veteran cowboy on the steps. Tomahawk looked like an impish child who had skipped school and then realized that he had nowhere to go.

'What you doing, Tomahawk?' Red asked. He hopped from his mount and secured his long leathers to the hitching pole.

Tomahawk looked up. His beard jutted at the young cowhand as he watched Drake dismount.

'I'm just sitting,' Tomahawk said.

'But the Lucky Spur sounds real busy,' Red commented. He rested a boot on the step beside Tomahawk. 'Listen to the bar girls singing. You oughta be in there singing with them.'

'I was in there but them bar girls are older than they sound,' Tomahawk said with a sigh. 'If'n I was drunk I might not have noticed, but seeing them with sober eyes was kinda sad and disappointing, boy.'

'Kinda old, are they?' Red looked downhearted.

'Yep, and half the Circle O boys are in there getting steamed up,' Tomahawk added. 'Give them critters another hour and they'll be looking for a fight.'

'Is that why you're out here?'

Tomahawk looked offended.

'It sure ain't. I could handle them boys with one hand tied behind my back,' he said, then added, 'as long as I had my trusty old tomahawk in the other.'

Larry Drake knotted his reins, ducked under the pole and followed Red up on to the steps. Both cowboys looked down on the scrawny Tomahawk as he toyed with the bottle.

'How come you look so glum, Tomahawk?' Drake asked. He pushed the brim of his Stetson off his temple to reveal a line of tanned skin, which did not reach his hairline. 'I seen you turn your gelding and slide off when we were driving the steers to the stockyard. I knew that you were headed for one of the saloons.'

'Is you implying something?' Tomahawk raised his bushy eyebrows. 'What you doing spying on me, Larry? Don't you know that me and Gene got an understanding?'

Red laughed. 'Gene understands you OK.'

Tomahawk scowled. 'You young whippersnapper. Gene never stops me paying saloons a visitation at the end of a cattle drive.'

Red laughed out loud. 'Gene don't stop you 'coz he never sees you doing it, Tomahawk. You're too darn fast.'

Tomahawk gave a toothless grin. 'I am kinda slippery, ain't I?'

'How can you look so glum when you got yourself a full bottle of Kentucky sipping-whiskey between your chops?' Drake wondered, pointing at the whiskey. 'I'd be as happy as a stallion in a corral full of mares if I had me a full bottle like that.'

The wily old-timer gripped the bottle's neck firmly as Drake leaned over him. 'Go away, Larry. I ain't sharing no whiskey with you.'

'But me and Red are your pals,' Drake said with a smile. 'Bosom buddies, you might say. Surely we deserve a drink of your fine whiskey?'

'No you don't,' Tomahawk said. 'And if you had bosoms I'd still not give you a drink.'

'How come you ain't opened it yet?' Red asked, pointing at the paper seal over the cork. 'All you gotta do is tear off that bit of paper and pull the cork.'

Tomahawk looked angrily up at Red and opened his toothless mouth. 'It ain't so easy when you ain't got no teeth, boy.'

Both Bar 10 cowhands roared with amusement.

Tomahawk scrambled to his feet with the bottle still firmly in his hand. 'Quit joshing, you young galoots.'

Drake shook his head. 'I'd be real drunk if I'd spent me two hours with a bottle of whiskey.'

Tomahawk stepped down to the street and rubbed his neck as he squinted vainly up and down the long, busy thoroughfare.

'What you looking for, old-timer?' Drake asked.

'I'm looking for Gene,' Tomahawk

replied. 'He usually comes looking for me when I wander off. There ain't no pleasure in sipping whiskey if Gene ain't here to bend my ear.'

The cowhands then noticed a rider weaving through the busy traffic. Drake and Red looked hard, then recognized the horseman as he drove his mount towards the saloon.

'That's Happy,' Red said.

'What's got him so all fired up?' Drake wondered as he followed Red back down the steps to come beside Tomahawk.

Happy Summers wove his way between a stagecoach and a wagon, then leaned back and halted his horse yards away from his fellow Bar 10 riders.

'Gene's bin shot, boys,' Happy shouted at them.

Tomahawk's face went ashen. 'Is he . . . ?'

'He ain't dead, Tomahawk,' Happy said as he steadied his horse. 'Johnny helped him to Doc Harper's place.'

Red and Drake did not utter a word. They ducked under the hitching pole, dragged their reins free and threw themselves up on to their saddles.

Tomahawk watched as the three horsemen turned their horses and spurred in the direction of the doctor's house. The old-timer walked towards his black gelding, opened the flap of one of his saddle-bags and dropped the bottle into its satchel.

He pulled his reins away from the twisted pole and then dragged his skinny frame up on to the trusty mount. For a few moments he did not move as he thought about his oldest friend being shot. He stroked the razor-sharp axe-head and snorted.

'Nobody shoots at Gene,' he mumbled angrily. 'Not if'n they intends living, that is.'

Tomahawk swung his gelding away from the hitching pole and lashed the tails of his reins. The horse instantly responded to the prompt.

'Come on, boy,' he urged as the horse

gathered pace. 'Some varmints shot Gene.'

The gelding rode into the dust left hanging in the air by his fellow cowhands. Within seconds he had caught up with the young cowboys.

# 6

There was an unmistakable look of disappointment in Roscoe Martin's face as he settled down in the lavish barroom set just beyond the restaurant of the Grand Hotel. Martin was only one of three cattle agents to frequent McCoy when the trail drives arrived, but he was always the biggest spender. The thin man toyed with his wineglass as news of the bloody gunfight spread like a cancer through the expensive bar.

Martin's only consolation was that Adams had been wounded and so would not interfere with what he had been planning for months.

Hugo Kline was another of the Eastern agents. He had finished his expensive meal and was about to go up to his suite when he spotted his rival seated alone at a table. Kline carefully clipped the end off a cigar and wandered towards the thoughtful Martin.

The sound of the match being struck above him caused Martin to look up. He gave a nod and gestured to the empty chair next to him.

'Take a seat, Kline,' Martin said. He finished his glass of wine and poured himself another.

Kline blew smoke over his shoulder and pulled the chair away from the table. He brushed the tails of his coat aside and sat down. Kline had once been the top cattle-buyer in McCoy, but for the last few months he had seen the newcomer outbid him for every herd.

'You did well today, Martin,' Kline said, eyeing the agent curiously. 'Three herds and you managed to buy the whole lot of them. Your clients must be real pleased with you, but I wish you'd leave a few crumbs for your rivals.'

'It's not my fault that your clients don't pay top dollar for the herds,

Kline,' Martin replied, sipping at his wine.

Kline rested his elbows on the tablecloth and stared at Martin with questioning eyes.

'I just can't figure you out,' he said. 'I can't figure you out at all.'

'I'm an agent like you,' Martin said, smiling.

'You're many things, Martin,' Kline answered, adding, 'but you're the strangest agent I've ever met.'

Martin sat back in his chair. 'What's that meant to mean?'

Mine puffed on his cigar thoughtfully.

'Why would your clients allow you to pay top dollar on every herd?' he asked. 'It doesn't make any sense. There are three cattle agents in McCoy but you purchased every damn steer in the stockyards. You even paid the Bar 10 over the odds for their longhorns. Why, Martin? What's going on? What in tarnation are you up to?'

Roscoe Martin smiled. 'I'm just

doing what I'm paid to do, Kline. I'm buying cattle for the hungry folks back East. It's not my fault that you don't outbid me.'

Kline shook his head and removed the cigar from his mouth.

'I tried to outbid you three times, but you kept upping your bid, Martin,' the disgruntled agent said. 'For the life of me I can't work out what you've got to gain by doing that.'

Martin stared at his glass. 'I've nothing to gain. The cattlemen get chits and they take them to the Cattle Association bank. I never even see any cash. You know that, Kline.'

Hugo Kline rose to his feet and returned the cigar to his mouth. He paused for a moment.

'Did you hear about Gene Adams?' he asked.

There was a long silence before Martin answered. Then he nodded. 'I heard. He'll be fine, I'm told. He was just winged when he poked his nose into the Black Ace.'

As an old friend of the rancher, Kline was outraged.

'What? Gene Adams is wounded and you mock him?' Kline said through a cloud of cigar smoke. 'That man doesn't poke his nose into other folks' troubles, he's courageous. Adams got caught up in a shoot-out, but unlike most folks he didn't run. He stood his ground and fought his corner.'

Martin stared up at his rival. 'Sometimes it doesn't pay to poke your nose into things that don't concern you, Kline. It might be wise to remember that.'

Hugo Kline frowned. He turned and walked away from the man seated at the table. As he reached the lobby he was wondering whether he had just been threatened or warned.

He paused and glanced back briefly at Martin. The smile on Martin's face troubled Kline but, no matter how hard he thought about it, he was unable to work out why.

Kline continued on to the staircase,

muttering under his breath: 'If I don't get a successful bid for the next herd that comes to town I'll be forced to relocate.'

No sooner had Kline disappeared from view than Martin finished his glass of wine and rose to his feet. He dabbed the corners of his mouth with a napkin and dropped a few coins on to a side plate.

He made his way through the plush barroom and hesitated at the doorway. A cautious glance at the staircase confirmed that his major rival had returned to his rooms. Martin inhaled deeply and swiftly strode across the lobby, collected his hat and left the Grand Hotel.

The Grand Hotel was set on a hill in the wealthiest part of McCoy. It dominated every other structure and just like the men who had built it, looked down upon the entire town.

Martin moved to the whitewashed railings that surrounded the hotel and rested his hands upon them. He studied the town, now bathed in the amber light of countless lanterns as McCoy prepared for the coming of darkness.

His eyes stared out at the very varied array of buildings below him. From his high vantage point Martin could see, over the opposite rooftops, the black smoke which pumped into the heavens from the stacks of freight trains in the stockyard.

Martin rubbed his hands together and grinned to himself. Everything was going in order, he thought. Months of careful planning was about to pay off.

He could almost taste the money.

The fortune which he had willingly paid to the Circle O and Lazy J for their herds had been far more than was usual, yet he knew that his Eastern clients would pay anything for the fine Texan stock.

Martin walked down the steep steps to the street. His knowing eyes could see the dozens of horses outside various saloons. He adjusted his hat and made towards the tall stone-fronted building at a fair pace.

McCoy was full to overflowing, yet not one of the thousands of people who filled its numerous streets noticed as Roscoe Martin entered the Cattle Association office.

Even if they had seen the cattle agent, none would have known what he was doing. Or why he was doing it. Only Martin himself knew exactly what his plan was and he was not telling.

Again he glanced around the streets but there was no sign of the mysterious rider whom he had sent for. He checked his pocket watch and closed the large oak door behind him.

# 7

The entire town was bathed in a crimson hue as the sun started to sink beyond the surrounding hills. Another day was slowly dying, as was its ritual, but this day was going out in style. Shafts of rippling red light gave the impression that the entire sky was alight. Every pane of glass in McCoy dazzled the eye with fiery reflections as the Bar 10 cowboys gathered around the steps of the doctor's home and office. The small wooden-framed dwelling, situated quietly in a side street just off the busy main thoroughfare, had seen better days.

As the last light of the day fought with the inevitable coming of night the troubled Bar 10 men worried that when the fight was eventually over, so might be the life of Gene Adams.

The Bar 10 top cowhands waited

outside the doctor's small home for a real long time. Each of them was silent as he patiently waited for news of Adams's condition.

News which was taking a mighty long time to reach them.

Since their arrival only the ancient Tomahawk had been allowed inside the old unpainted house by the equally aged doctor whilst he tended to Gene Adams's injuries.

The cowboys were tense. Adams had been in the small house far longer than any of them had expected. Happy rubbed his horse's nose and stared up at the red sky. It was getting darker with every passing moment.

'It's getting dark, Johnny,' he remarked.

'Yep. It usually does.' Johnny Puma sat on the boardwalk holding the reins of his pinto in his gloved hand as the rest of the famed cowboys milled around him.

Rip Calloway paused above Johnny.

'What's taking so long, Johnny?' he

asked his younger companion. 'Gene must have bin inside there for more than an hour. How come?'

'Closer to two hours if that sky is right,' Larry Drake said wistfully.

Rip leaned over Johnny. 'What's taking so damn long, Johnny?'

Johnny glanced up at the tall Calloway. 'Damned if I know, Rip. Reckon the doc must be trying to sell Gene some snake oil.'

'You shouldn't joke at a time like this, Johnny,' Drake said nervously. 'It's unlucky.'

'Maybe so.' Johnny nodded.

Red Evans had not spoken for nearly an hour. He just leaned on a hitching pole looking across the narrow street at one of the other houses.

'What are you looking at, Red?' Drake asked the young cowboy.

Red rubbed his thumbnail thoughtfully along his jaw. 'I'm just trying to figure out why that house yonder has no drapes.'

Drake looked to where his pal was

pointing and cleared his throat. 'That is odd, Red.'

Red nodded. 'Especially as none of the females in there seem to have much to wear.'

Happy nudged Larry Drake. 'What's he looking at?'

'The house with the red silk covering the lanterns in the windows,' Drake answered. 'I'm gonna have to have me a long talk with him one of these days.'

Happy Summers drew the last smoke from his cigarette and flicked it with his thumb and finger into the sand. It landed a few feet away from half a dozen others. He moved back to the seated Johnny.

'I'm getting kinda troubled, Johnny,' he admitted. 'Something must have gone wrong.'

'Quit fretting, Happy,' Johnny said, and sighed without taking his eyes off his pinto pony. 'There ain't nothing we can do except wait. Doc had to fix that rib the bullet bounced off and sew Gene up. Maybe it was busted.'

The rest of the cowhands looked as worried as both Rip and Happy as they kicked dust off the boardwalk and chewed on their lips anxiously.

Then they heard the door handle turn. Within a mere heartbeat Johnny had jumped to his feet and pushed his way past the others to the door as it opened. The sight of Tomahawk holding his whiskey bottle made each of the dust-caked cowhands groan in disappointment.

'Where's Gene, Tomahawk?' Johnny asked the old-timer as he negotiated his way down the three wooden steps towards them.

Tomahawk paused and looked at the young cowboy.

'Where'd you think Gene is?' he replied. 'He's in there.'

Johnny leaned over Tomahawk.

'I know that, you old fool,' he hissed. 'We wanna know why he's still in there. What's taking so long?'

'Doc had to fix a couple of broke ribs,' Tomahawk told him with a shrug.

'Real messy. I ain't seen so much blood. Gene weren't bleeding, he was pumping.'

Red looked at the others. 'He'll need a fresh shirt.'

Tomahawk raised his bottle. There was barely a third of its contents remaining. He shook it and sighed sadly.

'Look how much of my whiskey that damn saw-bones used,' he grumbled. 'He was splashing this sipping-liquor around like it was water, Johnny. Hell, I like Gene but he ain't worth that much whiskey.'

'You mean the doc drank your whiskey?' Happy asked.

Tomahawk sneered. 'Nope, he just kept pouring it over Gene's wound. What a damn waste!'

'Is Gene OK, Tomahawk?' Johnny asked.

Tomahawk nodded and scratched his beard.

'Sure he is. He'll be fine but he gotta rest up. The doc said that Gene will have to stay where he is until tomorrow to give his wound time to heal.'

Red pointed at the house across the street. 'One of them females is waving at me. Darned if I recognize her.'

'Wave back, Red,' Drake suggested.

Johnny was thoughtful about their situation. 'I reckon that means I'm in control until Gene's back on his feet, boys.'

'Why you?' Tomahawk snorted. 'I'm older than you.'

'Everybody is older than you, Tomahawk.' Johnny pressed his nose against the old-timer's toothless face. 'Besides, I'm always in charge when Gene ain't around. You know that, you old goat.'

'What we gonna do, Johnny?' Red asked the young cowboy as the rest of the cowboys milled around him. 'Gene usually pays us our bonus money for the drive after he sells the herd. We're all kinda broke.'

Happy rubbed his chin. 'We ain't got enough money to rent us rooms until he pays us off.'

Johnny looked at the cowhands.

'We'll go to the nearest hotel and I'll rent us all rooms for the night, boys,' he said. 'Gene can pay the bill when he gets back on his feet.'

Tomahawk looked at Johnny and frowned. He shook his head knowingly.

'How'd you intend doing that, boy?' he asked. 'You ain't got no money either. They don't take credit in McCoy from the likes of us. Them hotel folks are kinda shy of cowboys.'

Johnny knew Tomahawk was right.

'Yeah, they are a tad ornery. What am I gonna do?' he asked.

A knowing smile lit up the toothless face of Tomahawk. He stomped his boot on the ground and stood on his toes to look into Johnny's startled face.

'I got it,' he revealed. 'You get that chit from Gene and cash it at the Cattle Aassociation and pay the boys. Then we'll be able to afford the hotel rooms.'

'And have enough left over to rest up our horses in the livery stable,' Rip added.

Johnny looked anxious.

'Do you really reckon Gene would let me?' he asked Tomahawk. 'Even though he didn't get the price he was expecting that chit is worth a tidy sum. He might not trust me with that money. What if I lose it?'

'You ain't gonna lose the money, boy,' Tomahawk said confidently. 'You got us to guard you and the cash. I'll go ask him and get the chit. When you got the chit we'll all head on down to the Cattle Association and cash it for Gene.'

Johnny looked doubtful. 'Are you sure he'll agree to this, Tomahawk?'

'Sure I am.' Tomahawk nodded. 'Gene trusts us.'

'I'm sure Gene won't cotton to giving you that chit, Tomahawk. He's wounded, not simple-minded.' Johnny rested his hands on his gunbelt.

Tomahawk ambled back to the door and paused as his scrawny hand turned the handle. 'He'll give it to me. I'm his oldest pal. He trusts me, Johnny. Young

Gene trusts me with his life.'

'But does he trust you with his money, Tomahawk?' Johnny shook his head.

Tomahawk pointed a finger at the young cowhand.

'Why, you cheeky young whipper-snapper,' he snorted. 'I oughta take a hickory stick to you.'

'I just don't like the responsibility of handling that kinda money,' Johnny said worriedly.

Happy patted Johnny on the back.

'Relax, Johnny. If Tomahawk reckons Gene will let you cash in the chit, then I figure he's right.'

'As long as Gene ain't got any objections then I guess it'll be OK.' Johnny shrugged off his doubts.

'Gene ain't got no objections,' Tomahawk said.

Johnny and the rest of the cowhands smiled as Tomahawk opened the door. He looked back at them. Then he gave an impish look at the Bar 10 cowboys.

'Gene ain't got any objections at all.' He chuckled. 'He's fast asleep.'

# 8

The Bar 10 cowboys had only just staggered out from the large Cattle Association building with a saddle-bag full of Adams's cash when the sound of rapid gunfire stopped them in their tracks. Each of the cowhands drew his gun as a dozen riders came into view. Tomahawk squinted and leaned into Johnny.

'It's just the Circle O boys, Johnny,' he informed the younger cowboy. 'They're shooting up the sky again.'

Two of the riders broke away from the others, steered their mounts up to the edge of the boardwalk and reined in. Joe and Matt Olsen were grinning even more broadly than they had done earlier that day. Matt steadied his mount and looked down on the cowboys.

'Where's Gene?' he asked.

'You critters look plumb naked without Gene,' Joe added. 'Where is that old galoot?'

Tomahawk screwed up his eyes. 'Gene's busy. He got himself winged earlier.'

Both the Olsen brothers looked concerned by the news.

'Winged?' Joe repeated.

'Is Gene OK?' Matt added.

'He'll be fine tomorrow,' Tomahawk assured them. 'Looks like you critters are headed home to the Circle O.'

'That we are, Tomahawk.' Matt Olsen grinned. 'That we are.'

Johnny handed the saddle-bags to Rip and stepped forward. He looked up at the two ranchers and pushed his hat back on to the crown of his head.

'Well howdy, boys.' He smiled as he looked at the two swollen saddle-bags tied to their cantles. 'Looks like you're taking your cattle money for a little ride before bedtime.'

Joe leaned over the horn of his saddle. 'We're going home, Johnny. We never earned this much money before and Matt's kinda nervous. We paid the boys off earlier. Most are staying here to drink the town dry but a few of the hands decided to ride with me and my brother.'

'Good idea.' Johnny nodded. 'Reckon it's safer to head on back to the Circle O with all that gold coin.'

'Gold coin attracts bandits the way honey lures bears,' Tomahawk said firmly. 'Take that temptation home, boys.'

Joe nodded and smiled as he focused on the bags draped over Rip's broad shoulder. 'I see you only got the one bag of eagles this trip, Johnny. At least it's easier to guard than all the coin we got here.'

Johnny smiled. 'You take care, boys.'

Tomahawk pushed Johnny aside. 'Where in tarnation are the Lazy J boys, Joe? I ain't seen hide nor hair of any of them since sundown.'

'They headed out about an hour ago,' Joe replied.

'They figured it was safer to travel back to the Lazy J tonight rather than stay in town with all their golden eagles,' Matt added.

'They made more than you did, I'm told,' Tomahawk said.

Both the Olsen brothers nodded.

'That agent *hombre* paid us a whole heap more than we was expecting. Reckon them Easterners got more money than sense.' Joe laughed, gathered up his long leathers and tapped his spurs. '*Adios.*'

The Bar 10 cowhands watched as Matt Olsen signalled to the rest of their drunken riders and set off out of town in a line.

Tomahawk looked at Johnny.

'I sure wish we was riding out tonight like them boys, Johnny,' he admitted as he watched Rip balance his bags over his shoulder. 'Guarding this much money makes me darn nervous. Them boys got the right idea, riding for home.'

'I know what you mean, Tomahawk,'

Johnny agreed. 'Usually we put the cattle money in the chuck wagon and ride with it back to the ranch. We'd better work out the best way to guard all that gold tonight.'

'Gene will skin our sorrowful hides if'n we don't,' Tomahawk added. 'Reckon we ought to go rent us a few rooms in the Sidewinder and bed down until sunup.'

'Good idea.' Johnny looked at the others. 'Take our horses to the livery, Red. You help him, Larry. We'll be in the Sidewinder waiting on you.'

Both hands touched the brims of their hats and headed back to where they had left their horses. Johnny then looked at Happy and Rip.

'Let's go find us some rooms, boys,' he said.

The four Bar 10 cowboys moved through the crowded street, making for the Sidewinder Hotel. As they crossed the street none of them paid any attention to the horseman clad entirely in black as he guided his mount silently towards the Grand. The amber illumination from the street lanterns glanced across Chance Taylor as he rode through the busy part of town and headed on up the hill towards the imposing edifice known as the Grand Hotel. Few things could have drawn Taylor away from his usual haunts but the promise of a fortune in golden eagles was one of them.

The hired gun stopped his mount before the hitching rail outside the magnificent hotel and surveyed the grand façade like a hungry man studies a menu.

Although Taylor was a deadly killer his boyish features belied that brutal fact. He resembled a choirboy rather than a man who had killed more than ten men in the previous three years.

Taylor looped his leg over his horse's neck and slid to the ground. He walked to the hitching rail and tied his reins to it. The sound of his spurs rang out as he walked up the steps to the large double door of the hotel.

The gunman walked to the doors and opened them.

His eyes darted around the plush foyer before he saw the man he had ridden fifty miles to meet. Roscoe Martin looked up from his newspaper when the jingle of spurs caught his attention. The sight of the man in black made the cattle agent smile.

Each man nodded a silent greeting to the other.

Martin rose. 'About time you got here.'

Taylor removed his gloves, tucked them into his gunbelt and led Martin away to a corner of the large foyer, where they could not be overheard.

The gunman stopped, lowered his head and stared at the floor.

'I came here when I got your wire, just like we agreed, Martin,' he muttered.

'The Lazy J boys and the Circle O have both headed out of McCoy,' Martin told him. 'They're headed on the same route as they used to drive their herds here. Apache Flats.'

Taylor eyed the few people who were inside the imposing hotel lobby before casting his attention back on Martin.

'I thought you said that the Bar 10 boys would be among the highest-paid ranchers,' Taylor said.

'They came in third,' Martin told him, then, slyly, he smiled. 'I made sure that Gene Adams got himself into a gunfight so that he'd be out of action and unable to interfere.'

'Good.' Taylor looked pleased. 'Adams and his boys are bad news.'

'He's bedded down in the doc's house.' Martin grinned. 'Got himself a real bad wound. He'll not spoil this carefully planned job.'

'What exactly do you want me to do?' Taylor asked.

'I want you to ride as fast as you can to overtake both outfits and tell Ben Gardner and his gang they're coming,' the cattle agent said. Carefully he folded his newspaper and put it under his arm. He was about to turn away from his hired gun when he felt his arm being gripped tightly.

Martin looked into the face of Taylor. 'What's wrong?'

'Buffalo Ben Gardner?' Taylor queried the name as if it were poison. 'Is that who you've hired to bushwhack and kill them cowpokes?'

Martin nodded. 'Yeah. That's what they call him. Why?'

'He's loco. That's why,' Taylor said.

Suddenly the expression on Roscoe Martin's face changed.

'What do you mean?' he pressed. 'I'm relying on that man to bushwhack the cowboys and bring the money to me.'

Taylor shook his head. 'There's only one way you'll get your hands on any of that cattle money and that's by getting it yourself, Martin. If Buffalo and his gang kill those cowpokes he'll head north again with every penny.'

Martin shook his head in disbelief. 'No. That's not the way I planned it,' he hissed.

Taylor moved closer to Martin so

that his words could not be overheard. 'Buffalo can't be trusted, I tell you. If you want to see any of the money you had them ranchers paid, you'll have to come with me and earn it. We'll have to reach them ranchers before they reach Buffalo.'

The thought of doing his own killing chilled Martin to the bone, but greed soon wiped out any moral doubts he might once have had. He nodded to his hired gunman.

'OK. I'll ride with you. We'll kill the cowboys before they ever get to Buffalo Ben and his boys,' he said.

Taylor nodded. 'Now you're talking sense, Martin. I'll go down to the livery and get us fresh horses. You be ready when I get back here. Savvy?'

Martin rubbed the sweat from his face.

'I'll be ready,' he said.

# 9

The livery stable was situated down-wind at the far southern end of town, far away from the delicate noses of the town's wealthier inhabitants. Shafts of eerie moonlight cut through its high walls of wooden planking and traced across the hay-littered floor. Dozens of horses were held in individual stalls around the vast interior of the livery, whilst a corral outside held twice as many less valuable mounts. Red Evans and Larry Drake had only just finished taking the last of their saddles off the backs of the Bar 10 mounts when they heard the sound of horse's hoofs approaching the livery.

Both the cowboys listened as the steady hoof-beats grew louder. Anxiously Red looked at his pal.

'I hear me a rider, Larry,' he said as he secured a rope across the front of a stall and patted Adams's tall chestnut mare. 'He's headed here by my reckoning.'

'I hear him too, Red.' Drake moved into the shadows beside the younger cowboy and pushed him deeper into the shadows of the livery. 'Keep quiet. The last thing we want is to end up like Gene. We don't know who this might be and there's bin a hell of a lot of shooting in town since the herds arrived.'

Red looked at Drake. 'I ain't feared.'

'Me neither,' Drake said in a low drawl. 'But I'm mighty cautious. We don't know who that critter is and we ain't gunmen. We're just cowboys.'

Red was about to speak when he felt a gloved hand cover his mouth. A fraction of a second later a long black shadow entered the livery as the horseman rode his horse through the large doorway.

Silently, Red and Drake watched from their hiding-place.

Chance Taylor dismounted swiftly.

'Blacksmith,' he yelled out. The two wranglers cowered in one of the vacant stalls in the depths of the large stable. 'Where the hell are you, blacksmith?'

A few moments lapsed, then the sound of heavy boots approaching filled the tall building. Taylor turned and stared out of the wide-open doors.

'I hear you. I ain't deaf.' The burly blacksmith walked into the livery from behind the gunfighter. He carried a long-handled hammer upon his glistening shoulder as he made his way to Taylor. He stood beside the horse and grunted. 'So what's so all-fired urgent?'

'I wanna trade this nag in for a fresh mount and hire another saddle horse and tack,' Taylor said as the large figure walked around the saddle horse. 'You have got fresh horses for hire, I imagine?'

The blacksmith stopped and glared at Taylor. The fancy shooting rig and its holstered .45s did not impress the big man. 'Sure I got saddle horses for hire, sonny. They're out in the corral.'

'Good,' Taylor said urgently. 'Can you go cut two of your best horses out?'

The blacksmith raised an eyebrow. 'You're in a real hurry, ain't you? I sure hope you ain't killed nobody.'

'I'm in a hurry because I have to be someplace,' Taylor said. 'Me and a friend of mine are late for a mighty important meeting.'

The blacksmith looked blankly at the gun-fighter. He held his hand out palm up.

'Money makes me work faster, sonny,' he grunted.

Chance Taylor pulled out a roll of bills from his pocket and peeled several of them off. He offered them to the unimpressed blacksmith.

'Is this enough?'

The big man nodded and pushed the notes into his apron pocket. 'It'll do.'

'Good. You go get two of your fastest horses while I take the gear off my nag.' Chance lifted his fender and hooked its stirrup on to the saddle horn. He then loosened the cinch strap and pulled the hefty saddle towards him.

The blacksmith gave another grunt and walked back out to the corral. Suddenly the sound of running filled the livery stable. Chance Taylor dropped his saddle on to the floor and rested his hands on his gun grips.

The footsteps echoed inside the high building. Then the cattle agent skidded to a halt outside the stable. He saw the gunfighter and raised a feeble arm.

'Taylor!' He coughed.

Roscoe Martin was panting as he staggered into the cavernous lively He rubbed the sweat from his mouth and moved towards the hired gun.

Taylor looked angry.

'I told you to wait at the Grand until I came back, Martin,' he said. 'What the hell are you doing here?'

Martin moved closer to Taylor and rested his hands on his knees as he sucked in air.

'I was nervous that you'd high-tail it and not come back,' the cattle agent said. He straightened up. 'This whole job hinges on us getting our hands on that cattle money. I had the feeling that you might just decide to double-cross me and ride on out after that loot on your own.'

Red and Drake could hardly believe what they were hearing. They remained as quiet as they could as Taylor waved a fist under the nose of his paymaster.

'I never run out on a job, Martin,' Taylor exclaimed. 'Besides, you promised to pay me two thousand bucks' bonus and I intend holding you to that.'

'I'm sorry,' Martin said. 'I didn't mean to imply you were untrustworthy.'

'So you should be,' Taylor sneered. 'I've killed men for less than making out that I was a lowlife. Just remember that when the shooting starts you'll be dead meat without me.'

Martin stared through the eerie light and nodded.

'Don't you worry. You'll get that bonus money and a whole lot more besides once we've ambushed them cattlemen. Do you reckon they'll put up much of a fight?'

In the unholy light that filled the livery and lit up the faces of the two determined men both the Bar 10 cowboys could see the smile that filled Taylor's youthful-looking face. A twisted smile etched itself across his features as he pointed at the cattle agent.

'Don't you go fretting none about them giving us trouble, Martin. They're just cowboys.' Taylor laughed. 'Nothing but stinking rich cowboys.'

Red and Drake looked at one another as they hid next to the tall chestnut mare. They remained secreted until the blacksmith had brought the two fresh horses from his corral and the two men had departed.

With the noise of their horses' hoofs still resounding around the livery both Red and Larry Drake moved out to where the blacksmith was getting ready to lead Taylor's lathered-up mount to an empty stall.

The burly man looked at the Bar 10

cowboys and scratched his head.

'I thought you two critters must have gone while I was outside,' the black-smith said as he patted the exhausted horse. 'Where you bin hiding?'

Red pointed to the far end of the livery. 'We were down there making sure our horses were secure.'

The blacksmith spat at the floor. 'As long as you're satisfied that your precious Bar 10 horses are nice and comfortable, I reckon that's OK.'

Drake and Red walked out into the mixture of lantern-glow and moonlight and started to make their way back towards the distant hotel.

Both were still confused by what they had overheard.

'Do you reckon we heard right, Larry?' Red asked. He had been ponder-ing over the conversation between Martin and Taylor.

Drake nodded. 'We heard right.'

'I don't get it.'

'I do.' Drake sighed. 'That fancy cattle agent Martin and that well-heeled critter got bushwhacking on their minds, Red.'

Red frowned. 'You mean they're after the Olsen boys?'

Drake nodded and added, 'And the Lazy J crew.'

'What'll we do?' Red asked the older cowboy. 'We gotta do something.'

Larry Drake rubbed his neck as he tried to think.

'Let's try and find the sheriff and tell him,' he said. He pointed down a side street to where a wooden shingle hung over a small office. 'There's his office, Red. C'mon.'

Both the Bar 10 wranglers ran as fast as their ungiving boots would allow. The side street was far emptier than the main thoroughfare and neither man met any obstructions. They reached the office and tried the door.

'It's locked,' Drake said as his hand rattled the brass handle vainly.

Red pressed his nose up against the windowpane and peered into the unlit office. He scratched his neck and looked at his pal.

'There ain't nobody inside, Larry,' he gasped. 'You'd think that the sheriff would be in town when he knew that there were a few cattle drives headed to McCoy.'

Larry Drake shook his head. 'Maybe the sheriff figured that with so many different herds headed here it would be a whole lot safer to be someplace else, Red.'

Red wandered around the boardwalk as his youthful brain tried to work out what they ought to do. No matter how hard he thought he had no answers. He rested his hip on the edge of the hitching pole and glanced all along the side street. Even in the lantern light it was obvious that few people, if any, were in this part of town.

'Where in tarnation are all the folks that live here?' Red asked plaintively. 'There ain't one lamp in any of the windows in this damn street.'

'Maybe they've gone with the sheriff,' Drake answered as he stepped down beside his friend. 'Some folks don't like the ruckus cowboys tend to make when they finish a long drive.'

'We gotta tell someone what we just learned, Larry,' Red urged. 'We just gotta tell somebody that the Circle O is ripe for bushwhacking.'

Larry Drake nodded and slapped the youngster on his shoulder. 'You're right, Red.'

'But who are we gonna tell?' Red asked. 'We gotta tell somebody and the sheriff ain't nowhere to be found. If we don't tell someone there's gonna be a whole heap more blood spilled.'

'Reckon we better get our sorrowful hides back to the Sidewinder Hotel as fast as we can, Red,' Larry said. 'Johnny will know the best way to handle this.'

'You're right, Larry.' Red nodded in agreement. 'Johnny will know what to do for the best.'

Both cowhands turned on their heels and started for the hotel. They cut through an alleyway and emerged back on the busy main street. They did not slow their pace until they saw the faded hotel sign.

No two men had ever been so grateful to see the Sidewinder Hotel before.

They leapt on to the boardwalk and nearly knocked the door off its rusted hinges.

# 10

The unblinking right eye of Buffalo Ben Gardner focused on the log cabin as he and his riders rested their mounts at the foot of the draw. They stared through the moonlight at the lantern light which escaped through the two small windows and traced across the ground before them. Jake Wells dismounted and knelt; his eyes studied the ground, then he glanced up at Buffalo Ben and the rest of the gang.

'What you seen, Jake?' Buffalo asked.

'This must be the route used by the trail drives to run their beef to McCoy, Buffalo,' Wells said. He grabbed his saddle horn and threw himself back on to his saddle.

Buffalo gave a knowing nod. 'Then this must be Apache Flats.'

One of the other riders rubbed his face.

'Apache Flats?' He repeated the name but it meant nothing to him or any of the others. 'What's so darn important about this place, Buffalo?'

The ruthless leader of the savage riders glanced at his men, then returned his attention to the hills before them and to the isolated cabin.

'This is where we're gonna bush-whack a couple of gold-heavy cattle outfits, boys.'

Wells gave a long sigh. 'That big old moon ain't gonna help us ambush no cattle outfits, Buffalo,' he said. 'We need cover to get the drop on cowboys.'

'We've got cover, Jake,' Gardner said as he pointed at the small structure on the hillside. 'That cabin will give us all the cover we need.'

The outlaws looked at one another; none of them dared question their leader's logic. Dust drifted from the hoofs of their exhausted horses as the ruthless Gardner started to smile. He dismounted and took three steps towards the log cabin that stood far off in the distance.

'That cabin looks over the only trail in and out of McCoy, boys.' He grunted and sniffed the air like an animal. 'From up there we can make sure that nobody rides in or out of that town without us getting our gunsights on them.'

The cabin seemed too far away to most of the riders; the heavily wooded land to either side of the cattle road appeared a far safer bet.

'Them trees to either side of the road look a whole lot closer to our targets, Buffalo,' Wells suggested. 'Is there another reason why you're so all fired up riding to that cabin?'

A cruel smile crossed Gardner's horrendous features as he placed a cigar between his teeth and struck a match across his belt buckle. He puffed frantically as his depraved mind thought of an even better reason to head towards the cabin.

'There might be.'

'There's someone up in that cabin, Buffalo,' Wells said, pointing at it. 'The lamps are lit and there's smoke coming out of that chimney stack.'

Buffalo continued to puff on his fat cigar. 'I know there's someone up there, Jake. I can smell her perfume from here.'

The mounted men vainly sniffed at the air.

'You can smell a female's perfume, Buffalo?' one of them asked. 'You sure must have a better nose than I got.'

Gardner pointed at the cabin. 'And she might be on her lonesome. She might be hungry for a real man. I got me a feeling that I ain't just gonna make me a pile of gold this night. I'm gonna have me some fun pleasuring a woman as well, boys.'

Wells leaned over his saddle horn. 'Are you telling us that we've bin hired to bushwhack a bunch of cowpokes, Buffalo?'

Gardner gave a nod of his head. 'Yep.'

'Who hired you?' Wells wondered.

The huge man gave out a laugh and

turned to face the most inquisitive of his gang. He glared with unholy eyes at Wells and the rest of his followers.

'I'll tell you who hired me, Jake.' He grinned. 'The most pathetic-looking beanpole of a man you ever done see. He was sweet-smelling and paid me to bring you boys here. His handle was Roscoe Martin and he was an agent for the Easterners. It was his job to buy the herds. He figured that if he paid top dollar for them cowboys' steers then it would be worth our while relieving them of their loot.'

Wells rubbed his jaw and grinned. 'And he honestly thought that you'd do his killing for him and give him a cut of the money?'

Gardner roared with laughter and slapped his thigh.

'He sure did, Jake. That critter was plumb pitiful.'

Jake Wells shook his head. 'And you ain't gonna split the money with Roscoe Martin, are you, Buffalo?'

'Nope. I'm gonna teach that witless

*hombre* a lesson, Jake.' Buffalo chewed on his cigar and returned his attention to the cabin. His unblinking right eye glared at the lamplight that shone out from its tiny windows. 'We'll water the horses and then ride up that rise to the cabin. I'll have me some fun before them cowpokes show, and if she's real nice to old Buffalo I'll not kill her.'

With a few well-practised waves of his hands Jake Wells instructed the other horsemen to dismount and water their horses. Then he tapped his spurs and heeled his grey gelding to walk to the side of the mountainous man.

'When do you figure them cowboys are due through here, Buffalo?' Wells asked. He swung his leg over his cantle and lowered his aching body to the ground.

Gardner turned and looked briefly at Wells.

'I figure they'll be coming through here anytime over the next few days, Jake,' he growled, smoke drifting from his blackened teeth. 'When the stinking cowpokes show themselves we'll be waiting.'

'We'll be waiting all right,' Wells said. He dropped his hat on to the ground and plucked his canteen from the saddle horn. 'I figure we oughta send a couple of the boys up the trail to keep a lookout. They can then ride back here to warn us.'

'Good idea, Jake,' Gardner said. 'That'll give us time to spring our trap.'

'If them cattle-punchers have sold their herds they must be toting a lot of money, Buffalo,' Wells observed as he poured water into the upturned crown of his Stetson. 'Any idea how much they're carrying?'

'I'm figuring it's gotta be more than twenty thousand bucks, Jake,' Gardner guessed. 'Maybe a whole lot more.'

Every one of the outlaws heard the words. None of them could even imagine that much money.

Slowly Gardner walked in a circle until he was facing Wells. Smoke billowed from his mouth as he looked down on the gunman.

Wells watched as Gardner's large hand pulled the cigar from his lips and tapped ash on to the moonlit ground.

'If you're a good boy I'll let you have what's left of that female when I'm through pleasuring her, Jake.' Gardner patted the outlaw's face.

'I'm much obliged, Buffalo,' Wells said as he watched his mount drinking the contents of the canteen from the bowl of his upturned hat. He rubbed his rear. 'This long ride might be worth all the saddle blisters after all.'

'When I split the money up between us I'm riding south into Mexico,' Gardner boomed. 'By my figuring I can live like a damn king down there.'

'I might ride along with you, Buffalo,' Wells remarked.

Gardner inhaled deeply. He looked at the other outlaws and then raged at them. 'You boys keep your eyes and ears peeled for cowboys. If any of you see or hear them I wanna know straight away. Savvy?'

'Keep your noses peeled as well, boys,' Wells added as he returned the stopper to the empty canteen and began screwing it back on tightly. 'Cowpokes got themselves a real strange aroma and it don't smell like roses.'

The outlaws laughed as Gardner glanced back at the cabin and lustfully rubbed the saliva from his mouth along his sleeve.

'Hurry up watering them nags, boys,' he growled. 'I got me a powerful itch and I know it's just gotta be scratched darn soon.'

# 11

Johnny Puma sat silently on the edge of the bed and listened intently to Red and Larry as they finished telling him and the others what they had overheard back at the livery stable. It seemed a far-fetched story and yet Johnny had a gut feeling that everything his Bar 10 friends had told him was the absolute truth. A pained expression filled his handsome features as he hung on to every single word the two wranglers were telling him.

'Is that exactly what them critters said, Larry?' Johnny asked the older of the pair.

'Honest Injun it is. Me and Red come running here to tell you what we heard when we couldn't find the sheriff, Johnny,' Drake said.

'I was real shocked when I heard what that cattle agent was talking about to that slick gunslinger,' Red added.

'I never did trust that Roscoe Martin,' Rip muttered.

Tomahawk moved to Johnny and looked at the fretful face of the cowboy. He wagged his finger under Johnny's nose.

'Well, ain't you gonna do nothing, boy?' the old-timer asked Johnny. 'Is you gonna just sit there?'

Johnny raised his head and ran his fingers through his hair.

'I'm thinking, Tomahawk,' he said.

Tomahawk screwed up his face and punched his bony right fist into the palm of his left hand. 'Thinking don't cut no mustard, Johnny. You gotta act. Gene wouldn't just sit there and think. He'd do something.'

Johnny sprang to his feet and wandered around the room. He knew that Happy and Rip were watching his every move in the same way that Red and Larry were.

'This ain't easy, boys,' he stated. He looked at the rest of the Bar 10 men.

'I'm in charge until Gene is back on his feet. I just can't lead you boys out after that cattle agent and his hired gun.'

Tomahawk walked up to the youngster. 'And why not?'

'I've got responsibilities, Tomahawk,' Johnny explained.

'You got what?' The old-timer raised his eyebrows. 'What the heck is responagilities?'

Johnny rolled his eyes and then pointed to the swollen saddle-bags at Rip's feet.

'I gotta make sure that the cattle money don't get stolen, Tomahawk,' he tried again to explain. 'I also got to look after you boys and not do anything dumb. Gene would surely whip my hide if I rode on out with you boys and we got shot up or robbed.'

'Eyewash!' Tomahawk sniffed.

'I can't do nothing without Gene's blessing,' Johnny insisted.

'Gene sure wouldn't do nothing, Johnny,' Tomahawk said. 'He'd not wait for them Circle O boys to get themselves gunned down by them back-shooting varmints. Gene would ride and try to help Joe and Matt before it was too darn late.'

Johnny was nodding in agreement. 'You're right, but what about Gene's gold coin? We can't take it with us. We might get shot up and then Gene will lose that as well.'

'I'm for riding after them galoots.' Red nodded.

'I'm with Tomahawk on this, Johnny,' Happy said. 'We should ride and try and help Matt and Joe.'

Johnny looked at the cowboys. He rubbed his jaw and brooded for a few moments.

'How many of you are willing to ride and try to warn the Olsen brothers?' he asked.

Each of them raised a hand.

Johnny bit his lip, then nodded firmly.

'OK. You win. We'll ride,' he agreed. 'With any luck we'll overtake Martin and his henchman and be able to catch up with Joe and Matt when they make camp.'

'What about the Lazy J boys?' Tomahawk wondered.

Johnny gritted his teeth. 'I reckon we'll never be able to catch up with them, Tomahawk. They lit out way too early. They gotta be close to Apache Flats by now.'

The Bar 10 cowboys gathered around Johnny as his mind raced. Every fibre of his being told him to do what Gene Adams would do. Finally he looked at Happy and Larry.

'You boys go and get our horses,' he ordered; then he turned to Rip. He pointed at the tallest of the Bar 10 hands. 'You stay in this room and guard them saddle-bags, Rip. Guard them with your life.'

Rip looked disappointed.

'Ah, Johnny. That ain't fair. I should ride with you. You know I'm good with my guns. Let young Red stay here guarding the gold coin.'

Johnny shook his head. 'Listen up,

Rip. The reason I'm leaving you to guard Gene's money is because you're good with your guns. Red couldn't hit a barn with a scattergun. I'm relying on you to guard that money with your life.'

Red Evans looked offended. 'I ain't that bad with my gun, Johnny. I've bin practising.'

Johnny pushed the gangly youngster out on to the landing. 'You can't even draw that gun, let alone fire the damn thing, Red.'

'OK, Johnny. I guess you're right.' Rip walked to one of the cots and sat down beside the saddle-bags. 'But I still reckon you oughta be taking me, though.'

Cantankerous Tomahawk shuffled to the door with his trusty Indian hatchet in his hand. He waved the battleaxe and made Red back away. The wily old cowboy chuckled and looked at Johnny.

'I'm ready to split some skulls, Johnny boy. C'mon.'

Johnny checked his own matched Colts, then followed the rest of his men out on to the landing. He paused and glanced back at Rip. He looked at his pal.

'You'd best keep this door locked up tight, Rip,' he told the wrangler. 'There just might be a few thieves left in McCoy who would like to get their hands on that cattle money. I know that none of them could get the better of you.'

Flattery always worked with trail-weary cow-punchers. Rip jumped back to his feet and gave Johnny a knowing nod.

'You can rely on me. No darn thief will get his hands on Gene's gold, Johnny.' Rip Calloway nodded and walked to the door. He closed it and turned the key in its lock. He sighed heavily and stared at the saddle-bags. 'This is all your fault,' he told them. 'I'll never understand how grown men can get so all fired up over gold coin.'

The tall Bar 10 man turned the brass wheel of the table lamp until the room was filled with its amber light. He pulled out a well-worn deck of cards from his pocket and started to play solitaire on the bedspread.

Then he heard the sound of spurs below his room. Rip walked to the solitary window, lifted its lace drape and looked down at his Bar 10 friends making their way from the Sidewinder.

'Sure wish I was going with you boys,' he said, and sighed.

# 12

Gathering black clouds began to drift across the large moon and the thousands of stars in the sky. Slowly, as the night wore on, a gloom began to spread across the vast terrain and to affect the riders who had started to ascend the steep hillside towards the cabin that was perched precariously upon its slopes. The silence was only broken by the sound of horses' hoofs as Buffalo Ben Gardner led his band of cutthroats up the incline.

Apache Flats echoed as distant coyotes bayed at the large moon far above them. The remote cabin seemed to Gardner to beckon to him as he led his band of trail-weary horsemen. As Gardner forced his lathered-up mount to negotiate the treacherous slope towards the lamplight that spilled from its tiny windows he caught sight of Jake

Wells raising his hand to stop their progress.

Gardner stared through the eerie light at Wells, who was jabbing his free hand at the air. Reluctantly the huge man pulled back on his reins and stopped his fatigued horse.

'What in tarnation is wrong, Jake?' Gardner growled angrily as he steadied his horse.

Jake Wells hauled his mount to an abrupt halt beside his irascible leader as the rest of the outlaws followed suit and stopped their mounts close to that of Wells.

For a moment Wells did not utter a word, but just gazed down from the hillside to where the treeline started. His keen eyes focused intently on the trees.

Gardner reached across from his own horse, grabbed hold of Wells's arm and shook it violently.

'Don't you see it?' Wells said, continuing to peer through the gloom.

'See what, Jake?' Buffalo Ben growled,

and he too strained to see through the moonlight as black shadows rippled across the ground below them.

'You best have a good reason for stopping me getting to that sweet-scented female, Jake,' he snarled. 'If you ain't I might just snap your damn neck.'

'I sure have, Buffalo.' Wells raised a finger to point at the densely growing trees that flanked the trail leading towards McCoy. Startled birds had taken flight as a cloud of dust drifted up in the pallid moonlight.

'Then spill it,' Gardner hissed.

'Look, Buffalo,' Wells said. 'Something spooked them crows.'

Gardner straightened up on his saddle and gripped his reins tightly. 'You're right, Jake. It looks like we got company earlier than we figured, boys.'

Wells glanced at the big man. 'If we ride down there we can get to the trees before they clear them. When they ride out on to the flats we'll have them surrounded, Buffalo.'

'It'll be a turkey-shoot.'

'Let's go pepper some drumsticks with lead.'

Gardner swung his horse around and drove his merciless spurs into its flanks. His exhausted mount started down the slope.

'C'mon. Let's get to killing them cowboys,' he yelled as his high-shouldered mount led the way back down the steep incline. 'I want them critters dead as fast as possible so I can get back to that female up yonder.'

Like a pack of timber wolves the outlaws tore through the night air towards the multitude of trees. They had the scent of easy killing burning at their innards. There was just one thing that could satisfy them.

The brutal slaying of unsuspecting innocents.

★ ★ ★

The Lazy J riders were unlike the crews of most of their rivals. They were all well-seasoned and none of them would ever see their fortieth birthday again.

The dozen cowboys of the Lazy J ranch were led by the bearded Jeb Jacobs. Feeling his age, he liked to make use of the chuck wagon's well-sprung driver's board, and he sat beside his cook as the veteran steered his two-horse team, trailed by the rest of the riders.

Like most men of his generation Jacobs had learned to survive by his ability with his gun. He had built his cattle ranch from scratch and had to battle with not only the elements but the Indians and Mexicans who had also claimed ownership of the land he proclaimed his own.

Yet there was little left of the fire in his aged frame any longer. Jacobs was a man in the winter of his life. Like those who worked for him he saw little future ahead and relished each day he was blessed with as though it were his last.

As the metal wheel rims of his chuck wagon slowly rolled along the tree-bordered trail towards the vast open plain known as Apache Flats, neither Jeb Jacobs nor those who travelled with him had any notion that they would never see the dawn of a new day again.

None of them would live long enough to enjoy their newly acquired wealth, for time, like the sands of an hourglass, was swiftly draining out.

The Lazy J riders trailed the rickety covered wagon out on to the well-trodden range like ducklings following their mother. Most slept in the saddle, allowing their horses to pick their own way over the trail.

Even Jacobs was more asleep than awake as the cook beat down with his long leathers and encouraged the matched pair of grey cobs to move onwards.

The aged rancher rested one of his boots upon the hefty saddle-bags that were lying in the box as he rocked back and forth, dreaming of the fortune in gold his herd had unexpectedly brought.

His dreams were to be short-lived

and abruptly shattered.

Like a pack of ravenous wolves the outlaws suddenly appeared on either side of the vehicle and horses. They struck quickly and without mercy. Their guns spewed lightning streaks of deadly venom.

The gloom lit up as one shot after another cut through the pale moonlight into the slumbering cowhands. The Lazy J riders dropped like the leaves of a tree in the fall.

Jolted out of his slumber by the deafening gunfire, Jacobs instinctively reached for his scattergun. He had barely had time to cock both its large hammers when he saw Buffalo Ben Gardner drive his mount in front of the wagon's team and level both his smoking six-guns at the driver and himself.

The wagon team stopped as the gruesome Gardner trained his scatter-gun on the stunned pair on the driver's seat. As both the Lazy J men stared at the horrific sight of the huge horseman staring over his guns they heard the relentless sound of slaughter behind them.

Flashes of light continued to light up the darkness.

Buffalo Ben Gardner watched as the startled rancher lifted his hefty double-barrelled gun. The outlaw gave out a guttural laugh and fired both his six-shooters at his two targets.

His bullets carved into them.

The bewildered cook dropped his reins, clutched his chest and fell head first from his high seat. At the same moment Jacobs felt a thudding impact in his guts. The double-barrelled shotgun slipped from his grip as his hands went to the savage wound. Jacobs clutched his belly and gasped when he saw the blood which smothered his hands. His watery eyes looked up in horror at the scarred face of the outlaw as Gardner pulled back on his hammers again.

Gardner's gloating smile seemed to reduce the distance between them.

Jacobs had awoken from a dream and found himself in a nightmare.

As he blinked in disbelief Gardner fired a second shot at Jacobs. The rancher's head jerked back violently and he fell limply across the driver's board.

A fountain of crimson gore pumped from the bullet hole. It continued to pour from Jacobs's deadly wound as Gardner steered his horse to where the body hung limply from the wagon. The ruthless killer stood in his stirrups, pushed the body aside and reached over the side of the chuck wagon. His long arm plucked up the hefty saddle-bags. He laid them over the horn of his saddle and swung his mount round violently. Blood dripped from the leather satchels as he drove his horse to the tailgate of the chuck wagon.

His cruel eyes stared through the swirling gun-smoke at the bodies stretched out on the ground. Even the eerie light could not disguise the hideous sight of blood as it glistened across the ground.

Gardner tapped his spurs and heeled his horse to walk through the brutal evidence of the short battle. With each stride of his horse's long legs the big outlaw laughed. As from his high vantage point he saw the bodies twitch, Gardner fired into the carcasses.

When Buffalo Ben Gardner was satisfied that every single one of the Lazy J cowboys was dead he stopped his horse, shook the spent casings from his guns and reloaded. There was no hint of any emotion in Gardner except amusement.

Through the acrid stench of gun-smoke Wells rode up to Gardner and drew level. Smoke trailed from the hot barrels of his own guns as he steadied his mount.

'We lost one man, Buffalo,' he informed the unconcerned Gardner. 'Shorty got himself plugged by one of the old varmints.'

Briefly Gardner glanced at Wells. 'I never liked Shorty,' he said pitilessly as he holstered his weapons. 'He was too damn slow.'

'He's dead now,' Wells said, and began to reload his smoking guns.

Gardner patted the heavy bags. The faint sound of gold coins came from the leather satchels.

'Good. That means our split is a tad bigger, Jake.' Gardner grinned ruthlessly. 'I wonder how much money we got here? Reckon it's a damn sight more than we figured.'

'I got me a feeling that the next bunch of cow-pokes will be heading on through here pretty soon, Buffalo,' Wells said. He snapped the chamber of his six-shooter shut, twirled it on his finger and slipped it back into its holster.

Gardner nodded and flattened his beard down with his large hands.

'You might be right,' he said.

Wells exhaled. 'Reckon we oughta move these bodies out of sight, Buffalo. We don't want the next bunch of cowpokes to get warned off.'

Gardner gave a throaty grunt. 'Good thinking, Jake.'

Wells turned to the rest of the gang. 'You heard Buffalo, boys. Drag these bodies into the trees.'

Gardner pointed at the covered wagon. 'You'd best hide that prairie schooner as well, Jake,' he ordered. He swung the head of his mount around and steadied the animal while his eyes stared lustfully up at the cabin. 'Like you said, we don't wanna warn the next bunch of gold-heavy cowboys that this is a dangerous place to ride through, do we?'

'It might be best if we stay here in case them cowpokes do show up earlier than we figured, Buffalo,' suggested Wells.

Gardner turned, stared up at the cabin and sniffed the air again.

'Yeah.' Gardner sighed dismissively. 'You boys stay here and wait for them cowboys to show up.'

'What you gonna do, Buffalo?' Wells asked knowingly.

Buffalo Ben Gardner grinned and spurred. 'Hell, I got other things to do, Jake. I still got that itch that needs scratching. It shouldn't take me too long to pleasure that female, though.'

'What if she's an ugly old hag?' Wells called out.

'What if she is?' came the reply. 'It's all the same to me, Jake.'

'I figured as much.' Wells shook his head and pulled out his tobacco pouch. He sprinkled the fine makings along the gummed paper and slid his tongue along its length. He tightened the drawstring on the pouch and returned it to his vest. His fingers located and struck a match. He cupped its flame and brought it to the end of the crude cigarette. Wells inhaled deeply and watched the smoke as it trailed from his nostrils. The putrid stench of death still managed to overpower the smoke, though.

The remainder of the gang watched as Gardner drove his horse through the gunsmoke up towards the cabin. His already weary mount laboured under the additional weight of the saddle-bags laden with gold coins.

Jake Wells looked at the gang and sighed.

'C'mon, let's get on with it, boys,' he said. He eased himself off his saddle and grabbed the boots of one of the dead cowboys. 'Let's clean this mess up and get ready for the next bunch of cowpokes to ride this trail.'

None of the outlaws objected. None of them dared in case the mountainous man heard their complaints and returned.

Buffalo Ben Gardner was more fearsome than death itself.

# 13

The Sidewinder was quiet, since most of the cowboys had left McCoy. So quiet that the lone Bar 10 wrangler was starting to get edgy as he sat on the bed and stared at the saddle-bags beside him. He toyed with the deck of cards as all bored souls do. He had played a dozen games of solitaire without success and had resorted to trying to spin cards into his upturned Stetson next to his boots. It was more than an hour since Johnny and the others had left the hotel room but to the caged cowboy it felt as though he had been trapped within its four walls for an eternity. He had been ordered to guard Gene Adams's gold coins with his life, but he was tired. Rip rested his head back against two pillows and yawned.

He closed his eyes and inhaled deeply as he fought valiantly against his exhaustion. A million thoughts filtered through his mind. He recalled rising before sunup and driving the herd of long-horns into McCoy. It had taken hours for him and the rest of the Bar 10 cowboys to fill the stock pens with them. Every muscle in his long, lean frame ached and begged him to sleep, but he refused.

He yawned again. Sleep was a powerful siren to ignore but the wrangler was determined to do so. Even if it meant remaining fully awake until dawn. Rip opened his eyes and thought about the vow he had given to Johnny. He rubbed his face and sat upright.

Then Rip Calloway heard something.

It was the unmistakable sound of spurs jangling as someone made his way up the flight of steps to the landing. Rip threw himself off the bed and rested his feet on the floorboards. He paused for a moment and listened even harder.

The footsteps continued on towards his room.

Rip jumped to his feet, dragged his gun from its holster and moved to the locked door. He held his breath and placed his ear against the paintwork of the door.

Somebody was coming, he thought. Were they the robbers he had been warned about?

As the room Johnny had rented was at the end of the long corridor it soon became obvious to the tall wrangler that whoever it was, he was headed for his room.

A bead of sweat trailed down from his black hair. Rip glanced at the saddle-bags on the bed, then pressed his ear against the door even harder.

The footsteps grew louder.

Who would be coming to his room at this time of night?

The question tormented the wrangler like hot branding irons. He looked back at the bags again. Johnny had ordered him to guard them with his life. That was exactly what he was going to do, he resolved.

If someone wanted those saddle-bags and the golden coins they contained they would have to kill for them. He pressed his ear against the door.

The sound of the spurs was even closer now, he thought.

Who would be calling at this hour? Rip wondered.

Then the walking stopped. Rip stared wide-eyed at the doorknob as it turned several times. Someone was trying to get into the room.

Suddenly the entire door jolted as a fist pounded on the other side. Rip almost jumped out of his skin. He moved away with his gun still aimed at the woodwork.

The wrangler grabbed the saddle-bags and tucked them protectively under his arm. His eyes darted around the room but there was no escape.

The door rocked again as it was pounded.

'Who is it?' Rip shouted, standing between two of the cots. 'I'm armed and dangerous. Go away or I'll shoot.'

There was a brief silence. Then:

'Is that you, Rip?'

The familiar voice burned into Rip's mind. He recognized the low drawl.

'Gene?' Rip called out.

'Who in tarnation do you think it is?' Adams said from the corridor. 'Are you gonna let me in or am I gonna have to buy a new door after I smash this'un to bits?'

Rip cautiously edged to the door. 'You're meant to be sleeping at the doc's, Gene.'

'I was until I recalled that scrawny old varmint coming in and taking the chit for my longhorns,' Adams said. 'I got a bit fearful he'd lose it before I had time to see my money. Let me in, Rip. I've got a bone to pick with Tomahawk.'

Rip turned the key and pulled the door open. He smiled sheepishly at Adams as the rancher marched into the room and looked around at the empty beds.

'Where's everyone?' Adams wondered, looking at Rip. 'More especially, where's Tomahawk?'

Rip closed the door. 'They all rode out.'

'What?' Adams questioned.

'I got your money.' Rip smiled and patted the bag under his arm. 'Safe and sound. We only took enough to pay for the room.'

Adams strode up to Rip and looked him in the eye.

'Where did they ride to, Rip?' he asked. 'And why?' The tall cowboy raised his eyebrows as his mind raced.

Rip thought about the question carefully, then frowned. The desire for sleep was still taunting him.

'Tomahawk was goading Johnny,' Rip said. 'It was his notion to go and try and warn them Olsens. He nagged and nagged him until Johnny finally gave in and decided it was the right thing to do.'

'That figures,' Adams said.

'Tomahawk reckoned that Joe and Matt were in big trouble,' Rip explained. 'That's why they had to catch up with them.'

Adams raised his eyebrows. 'And why would Tomahawk and Johnny want to catch up with the Circle O boys, Rip?'

Rip thought carefully. 'Red and Larry overheard that cattle agent talking with a hired gunman. They was talking killing.'

'Red and Larry overheard Roscoe Martin talking to a hired gun?' Adams repeated the wrangler's words. 'Are you sure?'

Rip nodded. 'I'm sure OK,' he said. He followed the older man around the room. 'They said that them rascals were talking about killing them Olsen boys to get their hands on their cattle money, Gene.'

Adams stopped in his tracks and glanced at the tall figure beside him. He was about to speak when he realized why Martin had bid so high for the two cattle herds which had got to town before his longhorns.

The rancher rubbed his chin and sat down on the edge of the bed. He toyed with the playing cards thoughtfully.

'Martin did pay well over the going rate for the Lazy J steers as well as Joe's and Matt's whitefaced cattle, come to think about it,' Adams drawled. 'And you say that Red and Larry overheard Martin talking with a gunman?'

'They sure did,' Rip affirmed. 'Down at the livery. They tried to tell the sheriff but they couldn't even find the critter.'

Adams touched his side. The wound was still giving him grief. His eyes looked around the room.

'I wonder if Martin had anything to do with me getting shot?' he mused.

Rip leaned over the rancher. 'I figure them critters you and Johnny tangled with must have been trying to get you into a fight, Gene.'

The rancher looked at Rip. 'Why?'

'The sheriff is out of town and them critters you fought with weren't belonging to any of the trail-drive crews,' Rip stated. 'I asked around town and nobody had ever seen them before.

Martin might have hired them as well. The strangers started shooting and you charged in to stop them. Maybe that was part of a plan? They suckered you and Johnny but didn't figure on you boys being good with your guns.'

'You might be right.' Adams nodded.

'The spider and the fly, Gene,' Rip said. 'Maybe Martin figured that you might prove a problem and he wanted you out of the way.'

Gene Adams stood back up as a chilling thought came to him. He grabbed Rip's arm.

'You said Johnny and the others rode out after the Olsen boys,' he stated. 'How long have they bin gone, boy?'

'About an hour or so.'

Adams walked uncomfortably to the window and stared down into the amber-lit street. For a few seconds he said nothing, then he turned and looked at the wrangler.

'Get our horses, Rip,' he said drily.

'Why, Gene?' the wrangler asked.

'You can't go riding in your condition. You gotta rest.'

Adams looked at Rip. His eyes narrowed.

'Get your gelding and my mare,' he insisted. 'We're riding to try and catch up with our boys before they get themselves killed.'

'But, Gene — '

'Don't argue,' Adams insisted. 'I'm riding and that's that.'

'But you're hurt,' Rip said.

'The doc sewed and strapped my ribs up,' Adams said. 'I'm fine.'

Rip looked at the saddle-bags under his arm. 'What about this money, Gene? We can't leave it here and it's too darn heavy to take with us.'

'We'll drop it at the Cattleman's Association for safe keeping, Rip,' Adams said. 'Now get going, boy. Run and get our horses as fast as them damn long legs will carry you.'

The cowhand nodded firmly.

'Right away, boss.' Rip tossed the hefty bags on to the bed, grabbed his hat and opened the door. 'I'll go get our horses.'

The hurrying boots echoed around the narrow corridor as Rip raced from the room to the livery as Adams had ordered. Within seconds the sound of the wrangler's spurs could be heard out in the street as Rip ran for the distant livery stable.

The Bar 10 rancher gritted his teeth as he rested a hand on his ribs. He was in a lot more discomfort than he would ever admit, but he knew that there was something more important than his own pain.

It was the lives of his precious riders.

Adams had to try and catch up with them. He had to try and stop them from ending up as dead as the two men whom he and Johnny had fought earlier.

The Bar 10 rancher stepped away from the window and stared at the playing card in his gloved hand. He looked at it and then flicked it on to the bed.

The card spun through the air.
It landed face up on the saddle-bags.
The rancher stared down at it.

'The ace of spades,' Gene Adams noted. 'Good job I ain't superstitious.'

# 14

Roscoe Martin hung on to the saddle horn as he trailed Chance Taylor through the heavily wooded pass. Both riders had made good time in their quest to catch up with the Circle O cowboys and get their hands on the small fortune in gold coins they had been paid for their herd of whitefaced cattle. The ruthless gunman led the pair along the wide trail flanked by trees. Then Taylor slowed his horse, allowing his paymaster to draw level with him. The keen instincts of the hired gun sensed that they were now close to their objective.

The flickering light from a campfire danced between the trees and brush. Taylor grabbed hold of his cohort's bridle and abruptly stopped the mount.

'What's going on?' Martin gasped. The cattle agent somehow managed to stay upon the horse as Taylor raised a finger to his lips.

'Reckon we've caught up with the Circle O crew, Martin,' Taylor whispered. He swung a leg over his cantle and dropped to the ground. He helped Martin dismount, then tied the reins of each of them to a tree branch.

Martin rubbed his crotch. 'Don't they make narrower horses?'

'Hush the hell up, Martin.' Taylor pressed the palm of his hand against the cattle agent's mouth and dragged him by the collar through the dense undergrowth. 'Look yonder.'

Martin blinked and stared over the hand against his face. Then he saw the light from the campfire as Taylor had done moments earlier.

'Is that them?' he asked.

'Reckon it must be,' Taylor coldly replied. 'Let's go find out for sure. C'mon.'

Both men walked through the trees for about a quarter of a mile until they reached a clearing to the side of the trail. The smell of burning wood filled their nostrils as they watched the cowboys gathered around the fire. Taylor pointed through the brush at the cowboys.

'They're ripe for killing by my reckoning, Martin.'

Martin screwed up his eyes and peered through the dense foliage at the Circle O men. The agent looked at the cowboys' line of horses tied to branches just beyond their saddles and bedrolls. Their bedrolls were laid out around the roaring campfire in a circle. Three of the cowboys had already bedded down whilst the Olsen brothers sat close to one another as they sucked on expensive cigars.

Taylor and Martin could hear the brothers laughing as they shared a bottle of whiskey. The gunslinger moved slightly forward and stared around the makeshift campsite.

Then a smile etched itself across his deceptively youthful face. He smiled and pointed at the swollen saddle-bags next to Matt Olsen's saddle.

'Reckon that must be where they got the gold coin stashed, Martin,' Taylor whispered.

Martin squinted and nodded in silent agreement.

The sound of a howling wolf traced through the wood. Neither of the cowboys seemed to notice as they continued drinking and enjoying their cigars.

'Draw your gun, Martin,' Taylor said quietly as he drew both his own weapons.

'What?' The gravity of what they were about to do suddenly dawned on Roscoe Martin. He swallowed hard and reached for the newly acquired holster on his hip. He found the equally pristine .45 and pulled it free. He stared at the deadly weapon in his shaking hand.

'Have you ever fired a gun before?' Taylor asked his paymaster.

Martin shook his head. 'Of course not.'

Taylor sighed. 'Then be darn careful. I don't fancy being shot by you.'

'How are we going to do this?' Martin asked the far more experienced gunman.

Taylor pushed the six-shooter aside. 'Don't shoot unless I'm well out of the way. Savvy?'

Martin nodded feebly. 'I . . . I savvy.'

The gunman looked carefully around the area. The light of the moon did not reach the small clearing beside the trail road. The only source of any light at all was the blazing campfire.

Eerie red-and-white reflected flames danced over the two Olsen boys as they sat joking with one another. Taylor narrowed his eyes and gripped his guns. He jerked his head in a silent signal to follow.

Like a faithful hound, Martin followed.

Taylor led his paymaster through the undergrowth until they were directly behind their chosen targets. The laughing cowboys were blissfully unaware that there were two men behind them. A sly smile appeared on Taylor's handsome face.

His almost childlike features somehow altered as the light of the blazing campfire danced across his face. Now Chance Taylor looked exactly like all men of his profession when they are contemplating their next kill.

He turned and whispered to Martin.

'Keep that gun aimed at the ground,' he ordered. 'I'll do the killing. I don't wanna get killed by a greenhorn.'

Now the light of the campfire danced upon Martin's terrified face. He nodded. He was scared and it showed. The cattle agent had never imagined that he would be required to join the killer in the execution of his savage slaughtering.

Taylor stepped towards his targets with both his guns cocked in his hands. He moved silently and with deadly purpose towards the cowboys.

With each step he closed the distance between the Circle O boys and his levelled weaponry. Taylor was within ten feet of his chosen targets when Martin clumsily stumbled and stepped on a dry twig.

The clearing resounded with the snap.

Within a heartbeat both Joe and Matt had jumped to their feet as they reacted to the unexpected noise. Both the cowboys swung around and saw the two men bathed in the light of the campfire.

For an endless instant the Olsens and Taylor just stared at each other. Then Martin tripped and fell forward. As the hapless cattle agent landed on his knees his gun blasted into the ground. A huge plume of dust kicked up from the ground.

'What in tarnation?' Joe blurted.

Matt pointed at Martin. 'What the hell are you doing here, Roscoe?'

There was no time for the cattle agent to reply.

All he could do was watch in stunned horror as Taylor suddenly pulled on his triggers.

Shafts of deadly lightning hurtled from the barrels of his guns in quick succession. The gunman watched as both the brothers were jolted back by the sudden impact of lead hitting them. Without a moment's hesitation Taylor repeated the lethal action again. Two more plumes of venom rocketed from his gun barrels. Joe and Matt fell backwards into the flames of the campfire.

Even before the slumbering cow-hands had time to rise from under their blankets Taylor mercilessly aimed and fired his guns into them. Tufts of blackened wool exploded into the air from the blankets. Moments later crimson gore streamed from the bullet holes. Taylor did not stop firing until the blankets were torn to ribbons. He paused and lowered his head, his eyes darting from one blood-covered blanket to the next.

It was all over in less than a minute.

Chance Taylor stood in the spilled blood and watched until he was satisfied that they were all dead. He looked over his shoulder at Martin as the startled cattle agent got back to his feet, still holding his smoking gun in his shaking hand.

'I'm sorry, Taylor,' he stammered.

'You can holster that gun now, Martin,' Taylor spat as his expert fingers pulled the spent brass casings from his own guns before discarding them. With cold-blooded calmness he slid fresh ammunition into the vacant chambers. 'Reckon I oughta be thankful you didn't shoot me when you tripped over your own feet.'

Few men who had witnessed such horror ever looked quite so sickly as Martin when he staggered towards the carnage. His eyes widened in shock.

'Are they dead?' Martin managed to ask.

Taylor holstered his guns. 'Yep, the deadly deed is done. No thanks to you.'

Roscoe Martin swallowed hard again. He felt as though he was going to be sick but somehow managed to reach his partner in crime. He inhaled deeply and then looked down at the swollen leather bags full of golden coins. This was the reason he had hired the killer in the first place. He glanced at the baby-faced executioner in terrified awe.

'I've never seen such shooting,' Martin managed to say. 'You just killed the whole bunch of them as easy as most folks swat flies.'

Taylor's gaze darted to the pale-faced Martin.

'For a moment there I thought you'd shot me, Martin,' he raged. 'That shot you fired might have warned these cowpokes before I had a chance to pull on my triggers.'

Martin held his hand before his mouth. 'I tripped.'

'When you stepped on that branch you almost killed the both of us. I was gonna kill them fast and neat, but when you startled them I had to fire faster than I like.' Taylor studied the two bodies stretched out across the roaring fire. 'This is plumb ugly, Martin. Look at them.'

Finally Martin felt his guts churning and he had to turn away. The stench of vomit filled the clearing as Taylor lifted the heavy saddle-bags and balanced them over his shoulder.

'Leastways we got this.' Taylor smiled.

When Martin had wiped his mouth across his sleeve he saw the gunman staring hard at him. There was a strange coldness in Taylor's eyes which belied his smile.

'What you smiling about, Taylor?' Martin wondered.

'Change of plan,' Taylor said, patting the bags.

Roscoe Martin blinked hard and watched as the lethal gunman stepped over the saddle and walked back towards where they had left their horses.

'What do you mean by a change of plan?' he asked, stepping after the gunman.

Chance Taylor tilted his head and looked at Martin from beneath the brim of his Stetson.

'Like I told you, Martin. There's bin a change of plan,' he repeated. 'I had to work a lot harder than I figured. Killing don't come cheap.'

'What do you mean, Taylor?' Martin asked again, trying to keep pace with the hired gun.

Taylor did not stop striding back to where they had left their horses. He glanced over his shoulder.

'We've got us a new plan, Martin,' the gunfighter said from the corner of his mouth. 'I'm taking half the loot because I earned it.'

'Half?' Martin stopped in his tracks and shouted, 'You can't do that. We had an agreement.'

Taylor stopped and turned. There was a chilling look in his face. It was one which Martin had never seen before. Taylor rested his hands on his holstered guns and glared at the shorter man.

'Our agreement is null and void. You almost got me killed, Martin,' Taylor sneered. 'I deserve half and that's what I'm taking. Half.'

'You can't do that.'

Taylor smirked. 'Accept it, Martin. I'm taking half and you're lucky I don't take even more.'

Martin was furious. 'Half? We'll see about that.'

Taylor shook his head as Martin fumbled for his gun. 'Don't do that, Martin. Don't make me draw on you as well.'

'You ain't getting half,' Martin screamed as he managed to pull his .45 free of its holster. He tried to pull back on its hammer.

In one swift movement Chance Taylor drew, cocked and fired his six-shooter. The lethal lead cut through the night air and hit the cattle agent in his chest. Martin staggered backwards and watched as another rod of light tore through a ring of smoke from Taylor's gun barrel. The cattle agent did not see anything after that bullet hit him.

The gunman watched as Martin fell on to his back.

'Correction.' Taylor smiled at the lifeless body. 'I meant all of the money.'

He dropped the gun into its holster and continued walking on towards their two awaiting horses. With each step he kept thinking about the money that Martin had ensured the Lazy J rancher would get for his herd.

More money than he had paid the Circle O.

A lot more money.

He reached the two horses and realized that now Roscoe Martin was dead he had a packhorse.

Taylor secured the saddle-bags to the spare horse. As he stepped into his stirrup and mounted the horse a devilish idea occurred to the ruthless killer. He looked at the bags full of golden eagles laden across the mount vacated by Roscoe Martin.

Buffalo Ben Gardner and his gang were somewhere ahead, he thought. By now they had probably killed the other cowboys and got their hands on the gold.

Taylor looked at the bags and then at the trail.

A grin filled his youthful-looking face. Only a madman would attempt to get the better of Gardner and his followers, he told himself.

His smile grew even wider.

'Look out, Ben Gardner!' Taylor shouted at the top of his voice. He jabbed his spurs and started along the trail towards Apache Flats. 'There's a buffalo hunter headed your way.'

# 15

The sound of the distant gunfire washed over Apache Flats as Buffalo Ben Gardner returned from the small cabin. His unblinking right eye, not covered by the black hair that grew over most of his visage, gazed at the faces of his gang as he dragged back on his reins and brought his handsome mount to a halt.

Gardner dismounted and tossed his reins to the nearest of his men. He lumbered towards Wells, who was standing among the trees. He stopped and rested his huge hand on the trunk of an oak and gazed up the cattle trail.

Wells glanced at Gardner. 'Did you hear them shots, Buffalo?'

'Yep,' the large figure grunted. 'I heard them just as I got on my horse. Who do you figure was shooting, Jake?'

Wells rubbed his unshaven jaw. 'I'm

not sure, but whoever it was sure did a lot of trigger-pulling.'

Gardner withdrew a half-chewed cigar and rammed it between his blackened teeth.

'Yeah, that weren't no cowboys letting off steam.'

'Sounded like a gunfight to me,' Wells suggested. 'One hell of a gunfight.'

Gardner looked troubled as he turned his huge body away from the tree and stood thoughtfully staring at the hefty saddle-bags laid across the neck and shoulders of his mount.

Wells stepped to the side of the big outlaw. 'What you thinking about, Buffalo?'

'I'm thinking about us high-tailing it for the border,' Gardner admitted. 'That shooting has gotten me thinking.'

'What you thinking about?' Wells pressed. 'I thought you were set on relieving them cow-punchers of their gold just like we did to the last bunch.'

Buffalo Ben rubbed his wide neck. He glanced down at the smaller man.

'Them cowboys are meant to be travelling back to their ranch, Jake. We just heard a battle down the trail.'

'I know,' Wells agreed. 'It don't make any sense.'

'No sense at all,' Gardner grunted. 'Somebody was doing a lot of shooting. Why would cowboys waste ammunition in the middle of the night like that, Jake?'

Jake Wells began to realize what his leader meant.

'They wouldn't,' he said.

Gardner nodded. He struck a match and ignited the end of his half-smoked cigar. 'Somebody must have attacked them. Some dirty stinking galoots probably ambushed them just like we were intending to do.'

The rest of the gang gathered around their tall leader.

'If some other gang has struck at them cowpokes there ain't no point in us waiting here,' Gardner continued. 'By my figuring the odds are that we've bin crossed, boys. Double-crossed.'

'Let's ride, Buffalo,' one of the outlaws drawled.

'We should ride into Mexico like you said,' another added.

Gardner blew a cloud of smoke from his mouth and looked around them. His eyes stared at the moonlit flats which seemed to stretch on into infinity.

'I don't fancy staying here waiting for cowboys who might never show up,' he grunted. 'The longer we wait the more chance there is that the law might show up instead.'

Wells nodded. 'I've heard tales of Texas Rangers in these parts. They reckon them critters are even worse than regular lawmen, Buffalo. If they get our scent in their nostrils they won't quit until they got us hanging from a gallows.'

The outlaws all rubbed their throats as they listened to Wells. They began to mumble to one another.

'Who do you figure might have bushwhacked them cowboys, Buffalo?'

one of the outlaws asked.

Gardner stomped on the ground angrily. 'Roscoe Martin.'

'The cattle agent?' Wells queried. 'I thought you said that he was the most pathetic varmint that you've ever set eyes upon.'

'He is,' the big man said. He sucked on his cigar. 'But he might have hired another gang in case we didn't get here in time. I wouldn't put anything past that little bastard.'

'I reckon we might as well head for Mexico.'

Gardner filled his lungs with smoke and then tossed what was left of his cigar at the dust. He crushed it beneath his large boot and nodded.

'You're dead wrong, Jake,' he said. Then he turned to the others and boomed out his thoughts. 'Even if another gang has hit that bunch of cowpokes it don't mean we can't get that loot as well. I'm not headed for Mexico until I get the rest of the money Martin told me of.'

There were no objections. Gardner realized that they all knew that he would kill them all as mercilessly as he had gunned down Jacobs and his cook.

He turned and started back towards his horse.

Before he reached the weary animal Wells caught his attention. The big outlaw glared at him.

'You got something else to say, Jake?'

'Yep, I have.' Wells looked at Gardner as he stepped into his stirrup and hauled his huge frame on top of his saddle. 'I thought you said I could have the left-overs, Buffalo. You said that when you was finished with that female up yonder, I could have my fun. That's what you said, ain't it?'

Gardner gave a massive nod of his horrific head. His unblinking eye seemed to drill into Wells as a hideous smile emerged from somewhere within his beard.

'Well, ride on up there, Jake. I gotta tell you, though, that there ain't much point. There ain't nothing left of her worth having.' Gardner smirked. 'Nothing that you'd care to pleasure, anyways. Do you savvy?'

'I savvy.' Wells sighed. 'What happened up there?'

Gardner looked angry as he turned his horse.

'One thing I hate is finicky females, Jake,' he remarked. 'The sort that look at you like you were nothing. That woman spat, clawed and fought.'

Wells looked at the hideous Gardner. 'You killed her?'

'Damn right I did,' Gardner replied. He pulled his razor-sharp knife from its scabbard and waved its blade under Wells's nose. The blood-covered steel appeared even more gruesome in the moonlight. 'I gutted her like a fish, Jake. Nobody treats me like that. Nobody got the right to treat someone like they're dog dirt.'

Wells nodded. 'You're right, Buffalo.'

Gardner slid his knife back into the leather sheath and tugged his reins hard to his left.

'I'm going to ride down to that chuck wagon and fill my canteen, Jake,' Gardner growled. 'You make sure the boys are in place to kill whoever comes out of the woods.'

Wells rode his horse to a thicket and dismounted.

Every inch of his body wanted to flee. Yet like the others he was too afraid of the bullying Gardner to do anything except follow his mindless commands.

# 16

The five riders of the Bar 10 were gathered around the makeshift campsite just off the cattle road. The sickening scent of burning flesh had drawn them to the site of the scene of carnage like moths are lured to naked flames. Tomahawk had seen most things in his long life but nothing that could have prepared him for this.

The veteran cowboy stood like a statue, staring at the rest of the Bar 10 cowpunchers as they carefully placed the bodies of Joe and Matt Olsen over the backs of the Circle O horses and covered them with the bullet-ridden blankets.

As Johnny looped the dead cowboys' saddle ropes around the last of the Circle O bodies his eyes glanced across the smouldering ashes at the silent old-timer.

Johnny rubbed his gloved hands together in a vain attempt to rid them of the stench of death which had crawled into the leather. Happy walked towards the youngster, struck a match and lit a cigarette. As smoke drifted from his mouth he knew what Johnny was thinking.

'We rode as fast as we could, Johnny,' Happy told his pal as the cowboy brooded. 'There ain't any way we could have gotten here any faster.'

Johnny removed his gloves and tossed them on to the ashes of the fire. 'I know, Happy. It just gnaws at my craw that Joe and the rest of the Circle O boys got themselves killed like this.'

Red Evans was walking away from the gruesome scene when he stopped and called out in shocked surprise.

'Johnny! Johnny!'

Johnny Puma, Happy and Larry Drake heard the call and rushed through the moonlight to where Red was standing and pointing.

For a moment none of them could

see what had caused their pal to cry out. As the cowboys moved closer to the blood-covered brush they saw the body of Roscoe Martin.

'Roscoe,' Johnny muttered. He knelt and checked the lifeless body carefully.

'Is he dead?' Red asked.

'Sure he's dead,' Johnny replied. 'Two shots as neat as these don't give anyone the option of staying alive, Red.'

Drake shook his head. 'How come he's dead, Johnny? He's one of the varmints we saw and heard in the livery.'

Johnny rose to his feet. 'Maybe one of the Circle O boys managed to shoot him, Larry.'

'You're wrong, Johnny,' Tomahawk said from behind the broad-shouldered cowboys. They turned and watched as the wily old-timer ambled towards them. 'I checked their guns. Not one of them dead boys back there fired a single shot.'

Johnny moved towards Tomahawk. 'Are you sure?'

Tomahawk nodded firmly. 'Yep, I'm sure. Matt and Joe and their hands were killed where they was. They never even drew their guns from their holsters, boy.'

Johnny rubbed his face with his fingers and stared at the body on the ground.

'Then the critter that he hired must have done this,' he gasped.

Happy dragged the last of the smoke from his cigarette and then dropped it on the ground. His boot crushed it.

'He must have figured that if he kept the cattle money he didn't need Roscoe any more, Johnny,' he suggested.

Red pointed at the body. 'Roscoe got his hand on his gun, Johnny. He might have bin going to try and save himself from paying that hired killer.'

Johnny sighed. 'Only a locobean would try and draw down on a critter that earns his living by killing folks. Boys, I reckon Roscoe got what he deserved.'

Tomahawk shuffled closer to Johnny.

'You're forgetting something, Johnny boy,' he said.

'What have I forgotten, you old fossil?'

Tomahawk's unmatched prowess in tracking was known throughout the West. The wily old-timer could read each and every mark in the same manner that some could read letters. Johnny and the others watched as Tomahawk squinted at the moonlit soil.

'The tracks tell me that the hired gun ain't rode back to McCoy,' Tomahawk said, looking up from the road. 'If he had we'd have bumped into him before we even reached them dead cowpokes yonder. The varmint who killed them and Roscoe has ridden on after the Lazy J.'

'Are you sure, Tomahawk?' Red asked.

'Sure he's sure, Red,' Johnny told him. 'That old goat can't do much but he can read tracks better than most Injuns.'

Tomahawk raised his bushy eyebrows. His toothless mouth fell open as he scratched his beard silently.

165

Johnny narrowed his eyes. 'You're right, Tomahawk. That critter intends to do the same to them.'

Tomahawk nodded. 'Exactly.'

'I don't intend letting that varmint kill any more cowboys if I can prevent it,' Johnny said through gritted teeth. 'I intend stopping that critter.'

The cowboys all nodded in agreement with Johnny.

'You lead and we'll follow, Johnny boy,' Tomahawk said. He sniffed as he gripped the hatchet tucked in his belt. 'I'm ready to split his head a leetle bit.'

'We'll come back and take the bodies back to town after we catch up with that cold-blooded killer, boys,' Johnny stated. 'I figure he won't be making too much speed if he's toting the Olsens' cattle money.'

The Bar 10 headed back through the moonlight towards their horses. Suddenly they heard something coming at them through the dense woodland. The startled cowboys drew their guns as they listened to the sound getting closer.

'What in tarnation is that, Johnny?' Red gulped in terror.

Johnny bit his lower lip. 'Damned if I know, Red.'

Tomahawk pulled his Indian axe free and readied himself to throw it. The sprightly old-timer resembled a coiled spring about to burst free of its tethers.

'Keep on coming,' he muttered as the noise of brush being trampled came ever nearer. 'I'm ready to give you a mighty big headache.'

The five Bar 10 men stood in a line. They faced the dimness of the brush with determined courage. None of them flinched as they listened to what sounded like an advancing locomotive under a full head of steam.

Red was shaking in his boots. 'Holy smoke. It sounds like the devil himself is heading for us.'

'Easy, Red boy.' Tomahawk pushed the youngster behind him. 'Whatever that is, it ain't the devil.'

Suddenly two horsemen burst free of the dense woodland. They drove their mounts through the entangled bushes and emerged less than ten feet from where the line of cowboys stood clutching their weapons.

The five cowboys looked up in stunned confusion at the two riders. Tomahawk squinted and stumbled forward.

'Gene?' He questioned the evidence of his own eyes.

Gene Adams drew back on his reins as Rip Calloway came up beside him. The rancher rubbed the debris from his sleeves as his eyes glanced around the scene. The expression on his face changed from one of weariness to one of outrage. He tapped his spurs against the side of his high-shouldered mare and rode to the campfire. The chestnut mare shied away from the appalling stench.

Adams grimaced as he looked at the bodies tied across the backs of their mounts. Then he swung his horse around and looked down at his riders.

'Are they all dead?' he asked.

Johnny nodded his head as Tomahawk moved to the stirrup of his oldest friend.

'We tried to get here in time but . . . ' Tomahawk sighed and shook his head.

Adams nodded and held his long leathers in his black-gloved hands. He then spotted the dead body of the cattle agent. The half-light of a million stars danced across the bloody carcass.

'Is that Martin?' Adams asked.

'It sure is, Gene,' Johnny replied. 'We reckon he tried to draw on his hired gun.'

'That's never a wise move,' Adams said. He turned his mount and looked around the moonlit area. 'Any sign of the critter?'

'Nope,' Drake answered. 'We figure that he must have continued on after Jeb Jacobs and his boys. That's what Tomahawk says the tracks tell him.'

'Ambitious fella, ain't he?' Adams remarked.

Tomahawk looked concerned as he stared at Adams. 'What you doing out here, Gene boy?'

Adams forced a grin. 'Where else would I be?'

'In a sickbed, sonny,' Tomahawk snorted. 'That's where the doc said you had to stay until tomorrow, you young whippersnapper. You ain't got no right being out here with them stitches. What if they pop?'

'I've got every right, Tomahawk.' Adams turned his chestnut mare. 'Someone has to keep their eye on you.'

'How in tarnation did you get here so fast, Gene?' Tomahawk wondered.

'Short cut, you old goat,' Adams answered. 'I knew that me and Rip could cut more than an hour off the ride if we headed through the woods.'

Tomahawk looked at the grazed hide of their horses. 'It didn't do these poor horses much good though, by the looks of it.'

'They'll be fine,' Adams said. 'They still look better than you do.'

Johnny walked to where they had tied their horses and pulled on his leathers. He grabbed his saddle horn and swung up on to his pinto.

'Tomahawk's right, Gene,' he said. 'You oughta go back to the hotel and let me and the boys handle that stinking killer. Them ribs of yours might be hog-tied but what if they cut loose?'

'I'll be just fine,' Adams insisted.

Tomahawk sighed. 'You'd better be, sonny.'

Gene Adams swung his mount around and looked at Johnny. He pulled the brim of his ten-gallon hat down over his temples.

'Listen up. We've got to retrieve that gold for their families, Johnny,' he told the wrangler. 'We might even have to use our guns to get that money. I'm going, so you might as well quit gabbing and accept that fact.'

Johnny sighed and looked at the others.

'Mount up, boys. You heard Gene. We got us a killer to catch,' he said.

The Bar 10 mounted.

Adams looked at each of their faces in turn. He had never been as proud of them as he was now. The riders made their way on to the cattle road and headed towards Apache Flats.

# 17

Chance Taylor glanced up at the sky. Stars were disappearing as a pale glow spread across the heavens. Soon it would be sunup, the deadly killer thought as he rode up through the cattle trail towards the sprawling range. There was little that scared the lone rider, but he knew who Roscoe Martin had hired to bushwhack the unsuspecting cowboys on their way home. He drew rein and watched as his trail dust carried on towards Apache Flats. Taylor steadied his mount and pulled closer to the horse he was using to pack the hefty saddle-bags.

Gardner was the most loathsome of creatures, he thought. A killer who would do whatever he wanted to do because as yet he had never met anyone with the guts to stand up against him.

Buffalo Ben Gardner was a monster

of a man who towered over all those who trailed in his wake. The skilled gunman looped his right leg over the cantle of his horse and dropped silently to the ground.

Soon Taylor would use Gardner's abnormal size against him and fill him with lead. After all, he told himself, the bigger the target the easier it was to hit.

He led both horses off the road and tied them to the trees. The sunlight suddenly lit up the entire area. Taylor rested a shoulder against one of the trees and screwed up his eyes as he watched the end of the woodland.

They were up there, waiting. Taylor could sense the outlaws even though he could not see them. He pulled his carbine from its scabbard beneath his saddle and pushed its hand-guard down. He checked the magazine. It was fully loaded.

Taylor eased the guard back up and returned his eyes to the place where trees flanked the end of the cattle road.

Then he saw movement and nodded to himself.

They were there. Just as he had thought.

Taylor patted the saddle-bags that were lying across his spare horse and smiled to himself. He knew that Gardner never rode without at least a half-dozen gunmen in tow, but Taylor was unafraid.

The determined gunman rested the barrel of his Winchester against his left shoulder as his fingers curled around the weapon's trigger. He drew one of his trusty .45s and cocked its hammer.

'I'll teach you to try and bushwhack me, Buffalo,' he whispered under his breath as he set out through the undergrowth towards the place he knew the outlaws were waiting.

★   ★   ★

The rising sun was still low in the sky but its rays had already spread across the vast range where Gardner and his men had secreted themselves. Three herds of hungry steers had chewed its lush grass down to the dirt. Every inch of Apache Flats was baked a golden colour as the bushwhackers watched the trail.

Wells knelt beside the large Gardner. Both men held their guns and awaited the arrival of their next victims to emerge into the daylight.

'There ain't nowhere for them riders to hide now, Buffalo,' Wells said. He grinned as he carefully watched the cattle road.

'I thought I heard something a few minutes back, Jake,' Gardner said as he stroked his black beard. 'Didn't you hear horses a little while ago?'

Jake Wells shrugged. 'I'm not sure. I don't reckon so.'

'I heard something, Buffalo,' another of the outlaws said.

Gardner searched the faces of the rest of the gang. 'Did any of you hear horses just before the sun rose?'

The tired outlaws were unsure.

Gardner moved closer to Wells. His huge bulk bore down on the smaller outlaw.

'I'm sure I heard riders, Jake,' he insisted.

'Maybe you did, Buffalo.' Wells nodded. 'You got better hearing than any of us. Maybe you did hear horses.'

Gardner glared through the dust. 'Where'd they go?'

There was no answer to the simple question. For a few moments the crouching Gardner brooded on the problem, then he grunted and turned his devilish eyes upon the outlaws closest to him.

'Go see, Jake,' he growled.

Wells stared in shock at their leader. 'You can't be serious, Buffalo. If I head on down the road I'll be a sitting duck.'

Gardner pushed the cold steel barrel of one of his six-shooters into the belly of Wells. A monstrous smile carved a route across the bearded face.

'Go take a look, Jake,' he repeated.

Terror ripped through Wells as he felt

the barrel pushed deep into his guts. He tried to smile but it was impossible. He tried to swallow but there was no spittle left in his dry mouth.

'You want me to go down the road and take a look?' Wells asked fearfully. 'Then that's what I'll do, Buffalo. I'll go and take a look.'

'Good,' Gardner sneered.

Wells was about to stand when the sound of clattering horses' hoofs suddenly filled the area. Wells looked at Gardner and pointed at the road flanked by the dense woodland.

'Listen,' he said cupping his ear. 'Horses. Just like you said, Buffalo.'

Gardner stood up. There was a confused expression on his brutalized face.

'Something's wrong, boys,' he grunted.

Wells placed a hand on a tree and stared through the brush at the wide road used by the trail drives as they headed for McCoy. 'I can't see them yet but they're coming this way.'

The other outlaws rose from their hiding-places.

'Something's wrong, I tell you,' Gardner shouted at his men. He was trying to work out what was alarming him so much. 'That ain't the same horses.'

Wells looked hard at the befuddled monster. 'But you said that you heard horses, Buffalo. How can these be different ones?'

'I don't know but they are,' Gardner yelled out. 'I heard a couple of horses before sunup. Them's a lot of horses.'

Suddenly the unmistakable sound of a Winchester being cocked filled the ears of the outlaws. They swung round on their heels and saw the well-dressed gunman standing in the dense brush. The morning sun glanced along the metal barrel of his rifle.

Frantically the outlaws blasted their weaponry at Taylor.

Chunks of wood were carved from the trunk of a tree Taylor was using as cover. As a million splinters showered over the hired gun he began his reply.

Faster than any of the outlaws had ever seen before, bullets came spewing at them from the long barrel of Chance Taylor's gun.

Before the gunsmoke had time to fill the distance between them half of Gardner's men were either dead or wounded. The golden ground was stained with crimson gore as Taylor blasted again and again.

Jake Wells charged at the rifleman with both his guns firing at the same time. Taylor cranked the Winchester's mechanism and pulled on the trigger. A fiery rod of lethal lead erupted from the smoking rifle barrel and bored into the charging outlaw.

Wells was hit high. He flew backwards and crashed at the feet of the enormous Buffalo Ben.

The grunting Gardner cocked his guns as Taylor stepped away from the bushes. Both men sneered at one another as smoke trailed from their weapons.

'Who the hell are you, little man?' Gardner asked. His thumbs cocked both hammers on his .45s.

'Chance Taylor.'

Gardner spat at the ground. 'You got the wrong kinda rifle there, Chance Taylor. You need a buffalo gun to stop the likes of me, *amigo*.'

Taylor pushed his hand-guard down, then dragged it back up. Without a moment's hesitation he squeezed the trigger of his rifle again. The shot went straight into Gardner but the huge man did not flinch.

Gardner pulled on his triggers. Both his shots sent Taylor flying into the air and crashing into a lifeless heap.

Before the monstrous figure could inspect his handiwork he heard the riders again. He swung on his heels and saw Gene Adams and the rest of the Bar 10 riders thundering up the cattle road.

'Damn it all!' he growled angrily and ran for his horse.

Buffalo Ben Gardner moved swiftly

for a big man. He reached his mount within seconds and hoisted his bulk up on to the saddle.

He spurred just as the riders of the Bar 10 rode on to the range. The cowboys stopped when they reached the bodies of the outlaws.

Only the intrepid rancher continued to urge his chestnut mare in pursuit of Gardner. Adams gained on the outlaw with every stride of his magnificent mount.

Gardner whipped the shoulders of his exhausted horse but it was labouring. The sheer weight of not only its massive master but also the hefty saddle-bags made it impossible for the animal to obey.

Adams had to haul back on his reins when he saw the weary horse stumble and fall just yards ahead of him. The rancher stopped his mare and watched as Buffalo Ben Gardner rolled across the golden ground, away from his stricken mount.

Stunned and dazed Gardner forced

himself back to his feet and stared in disbelief at his horse. Then his devilish eyes looked at Adams. He dragged a gun from its holster and aimed it at the rancher.

'Give me that horse,' he snarled.

Adams shook his head and drew his own gun. 'Try and take it, friend.'

Both men fired at exactly the same time. Adams felt his opponent's bullet tear through his hat. Then as the gunsmoke cleared he watched the gigantic Gardner fall face first on to the ground.

As Adams sighed Johnny rode up beside him. 'You OK, Gene?'

'I'm fine, son.' Adams holstered his gun.

'I didn't think you'd be able to drop such a big critter as him with just one shot,' Johnny said.

'It only takes one shot if you hit what you're aiming at, Johnny,' Adams told him, and sighed.

# Finale

Rip Calloway rode on to the range with the two horses in tow that Taylor had left down the cattle road. Tomahawk squinted hard at the horses and then at the wrangler.

'What you got there, Rip boy?' he asked.

'I found these nags down the trail,' Rip explained. He patted the bags. 'This must be the Circle O gold coin that rascal stole, Tomahawk.'

'You did good, Rip.' Adams rested his hands on his saddle horn and surveyed the horrific scene around them. The sight of the bloodstained ground chilled the rancher.

Johnny walked around the bodies, vainly trying to see if any of them had survived the brutal battle. He walked to the mounted rancher and looked long and hard at Adams.

'You sure don't look well, Gene,' he said. 'You look almost as bad as these critters scattered all over.'

Adams rubbed his side. 'Reckon I'll bed down when we get back to McCoy, Johnny. I do feel a tad tuckered.'

Happy Summers looked around the scene of carnage. 'Leastways they killed each other and we didn't have to waste bullets.'

'We wasted one bullet, Happy,' Adams said.

'That was the best shot I ever done seen, Gene,' Johnny told the rancher. 'That was a bullet worth wasting.'

Gene Adams could not disguise his discomfort as he sat astride his powerful chestnut mare. He patted the neck of his trusty horse.

'Don't you go stepping in no gopher holes, Amy,' he told the horse.

Larry Drake held his reins high. 'Me and Red here can try and find that damn sheriff when we get back to McCoy. He can get these bodies buried.'

'When we get back to McCoy we can collect our money from the Cattle Association,' Adams said. He winced as he watched his men start to mount their horses. 'We'll deliver this gold to the Lazy J and Circle O families and then head on back to the Bar 10.'

Tomahawk looked up at his old friend. He could see the pain the rancher was trying to conceal. 'When is you gonna admit that you ain't as young as you think you are, Gene boy? I seen turkeys on the fourth of July looking better than you do. It's about time you rested up.'

Adams smiled and watched the old-timer mount his black gelding and gather up his reins. He leaned across and tugged at Tomahawk's beard.

'I'll admit it when you stop chasing bar girls, drinking rotgut whiskey and cheating at cards, you old goat,' Adams told his ancient pal. 'Is it a deal?'

Tomahawk looked like a rooster with its feathers ruffled as he thought about his friend's words. He turned his horse and winked at Adams.

'Deal.' He chuckled. 'Now let's get you back to that sickbed, Gene boy.'

'Good thinking, Tomahawk.'

The riders of the Bar 10 led their gold-laden packhorses from the crimson soil of Apache Flats back along the cattle road to McCoy.

We do hope that you have enjoyed reading this large print book.

Did you know that all of our titles are available for purchase?

We publish a wide range of high quality large print books including:
**Romances, Mysteries, Classics**
**General Fiction**
**Non Fiction and Westerns**

Special interest titles available in large print are:
**The Little Oxford Dictionary**
**Music Book, Song Book**
**Hymn Book, Service Book**

Also available from us courtesy of Oxford University Press:
**Young Readers' Dictionary**
**(large print edition)**
**Young Readers' Thesaurus**
**(large print edition)**

For further information or a free brochure, please contact us at:
**Ulverscroft Large Print Books Ltd.,**
**The Green, Bradgate Road, Anstey,**
**Leicester, LE7 7FU, England.**
**Tel:** (00 44) 0116 236 4325
**Fax:** (00 44) 0116 234 0205

*Other titles in the*
*Linford Western Library:*

## TWO GUNS NORTH

### Neil Hunter

Jason Brand's latest assignment takes him into the mountains, searching for two missing men — a Deputy US Marshal and a government geologist. But this apparently routine assignment turns out to be anything but. For Bodie the Stalker, hunting a brutal killer, rides the same trail. It's just another manhunt for him — until he finds himself on the wrong end of the chase. But then Bodie meets Brand. And when they join forces, it's as if Hell itself has come to the high country . . .

# GUNS OF THE BRASADA

## Neil Hunter

Ballard and McCall are in Texas, working for Henry Conway, an old friend, on the Lazy-C ranch. But trouble is brewing: Yancey Merrick, owner of the big Diamond-M, kept pushing to expand his empire. Then Henry's son Harry is run down through the brasada thicket before being shot in the back and killed. Determined to find the guilty party, Ballard and McCall suddenly find themselves deep in a developing range war . . .

# LONELY RIDER

## Steve Hayes

He calls himself 'Melody', after the word burned inside his belt. Because he can't remember his own name — or anything at all prior to the past six weeks. It's 'amnesia', according to Regan Avery, the woman he rescues from a fast-flowing river. But Melody doesn't need the fancy name for his predicament to know he's in trouble — for the few things he *can* remember involve being shot at and wounded, with a posse hard on his heels . . .

# GILA MONSTER

## Colin Bainbridge

A stagecoach is on its way to the small town of Medicine Bend when it is attacked by outlaws. However, the coach's passengers manage to repel them. This disparate array of characters — the new marshal Wade Calvin; Mr Taber, insurance salesman; and Miss Jowett, on her way to take on caring for her widowed nephew's children — thus find their lives intertwined. But as they settle into life in Medicine Bend, Gila Goad, the outlaws' vicious leader, hears news of the botched robbery — and is determined to get his revenge . . .